PAUL E. HORSMAN

THE SHARDHELD SAGA

Book 1

SHARDFALL

Cover: Jos Weijmer

For more info: paulhorsman-author.com

There is a glossary and a name list at the back of the book.

Paul E. Horsman's books:

Zilverspoor Uitgeverij (Dutch Editions):
Rhidauna – Schaduw van de Revenaunt #1
Zihaen – Schaduw van de Revenaunt #2

Red Rune Books (English Editions):
Shardfall - The Shardheld Saga #1 (2013)
Runemaster - The Shardheld Saga #2 (2013)
Rhidauna - The Shadow of the Revenaunt #1 (2013)
Shadows Under Nadril - A Revenaunt novelette

TABLE OF CONTENTS

CHAPTER 1 - SKYSHARD

It had stopped snowing. At the foot of the Silfjall Mountain, Eidungruve Hold lay exposed to the frosty blue of the Long Night.

Elward, the young watchman at the top of the gate tower, leaned on his spear. He stared at the crows, circling over the roofs of the buildings, while he waited for the end of his watch. After four hours on the tower, the cold was getting to him. His breath froze in his hairy face, forming icicles in his mustache. For a moment he thought of his wife below in the warmth of the longhouse. She was pregnant. He knew he shouldn't worry, but it was their first time, and it made him nervous.

He started pacing again, the snow crunching under his heavy boots. Six feet forward, six back, the length of his little kingdom.

Something flashed on the edge of his vision. Elward looked up and froze. A tiny ball of light hurtled down from the blue bowl of the sky. It hit the top of Silfjall with a flash, brighter than Thor's bolts. A terrible light engulfed him. He yelled, clutched his eyes, terrified by his sudden blindness. His spear fell to the floor with a thump. He groaned, half bowed, paralyzed with fear, waiting for the end. But the sparks before his eyes died and through his fingers the familiar Long Night returned. *By Thor,* he thought, still shaking. *I thought it was coming for me.* His fingers clawed the railing as he looked at the Hold. He sighed, the longhouse, the barns and the mine buildings beneath him, all were as before. He turned and his heart missed a beat. High up the slope of the Silfjall burned a blue fire. *Oh Gods, what's that?* With trembling hands, he sought the signal horn and blew a single, long note in the silence. The crows fled, cawing in distress, seeking shelter in the woods.

The headman appeared from between the buildings below. He started and stared at the glow on the mountain. Abruptly, he turned around and ran into the longhouse.

Elward shook his spear at the headman's back. 'Damn you, I'm up here, nitwit! I've got a report.' No one heard him. He glanced at the light, pulsing on the mountain like something evil.

The headman returned with someone else and Elward stiffened. Lord Holder Alman's wide-legged walk was unmistakable. For a moment, the men on the ground stared at the light and then they came up the ladder to his high post. The Holder moved slowly, as if his old wound pained him.

Elward slammed his fist to his shoulder in a salute as his lord stepped onto the platform.

Holder Alman nodded toward the blue glow. 'Where did that come from? When did it begin?'

'Only just now, Lord,' said Elward.

The Holder's eyes narrowed in their hollow sockets. 'Be precise, man. How long is just?'

'About half a watchman's round of the palisade,' said Elward, keeping silent about his moment of blindness. Stiffly, he made his report, conscious of his lord's searching gaze. He let out a sigh of relief when the Holder turned his head back to the light on the mountain.

'It is in the high pasture,' said the Holder. 'Is it a sign? But of what?'

Disaster, thought the watchman. He didn't dare voice his thoughts. The Holder would think it a sign of weakness and Alman hated weaklings.

The Holder turned to his headman. 'Send for my son.' Without another look at the light, he climbed carefully back down.

Kjelle stroked Ema's cheek and blew a strand of blonde hair from her ear. She giggled as he put his hand on her breast. Her pose shifted, as if she invited him to lie down next to her. His thumb stroked her nipple and she moaned. 'Yes, oh yes.'

His other hand pulled the brooch from her second shoulder strap. Swiftly he dragged both apron-skirt and shift down. Ema cried softly as Kjelle buried his face between her breasts. Her arms pulled him down on top of her. 'Hurry,' said she, as he started to roll up her long dress.

The door flew open. 'Holderling, your father wants you.'

Kjelle's face went from outrage to guilty shock. 'My father?'

The old freedman on the threshold nodded. 'Yes, it is urgent.' His eyes stared at the girl and he grinned. 'Very urgent.'

Hastily, Kjelle jumped from the bed and pulled Ema after him. 'I must go. Away with you.'

The girl pouted while she tried to straighten her dress.

Kjelle put his arm around her waist and half dragged her from his room. Chagrin colored his thoughts. *Damn, I almost had her.* His manhood moved at the feel of the chubby girl's body and he sighed. *Later.*

His father sat upright in the box seat that kept his valuables. Holder Alman had been a feared warrior once, till he got a spear in his crotch. That battle had been years ago, but the pain had never left him and he looked a shadow of his former self. Only his mind remained sharp as the dagger at his belt, and almost as deadly. Kjelle bowed his head, aware of the sweat on his face. Although he was a brawny fellow, his father still made him feel like a child.

'You have seen the light?' said the Holder.

Kjelle hadn't seen anything but the girl on his bed. Still, he gave a curt nod. 'Yes, Lord. '

Alman growled. 'Could you tear yourself away long enough?'

Kjelle clenched his jaw; of course his father knew of the girl. He knew everything.

Holder Alman didn't wait for an answer. 'A piece of the sky fell on our mountain.' The Holder gave his son a thoughtful look. 'You're of age now. It's time for you to prove that you're a man out of bed, as well. Take three guards and go to the high pasture. Hagen is one of the three. Use his experience and heed his advice. Stay on the path, then the snow will be safe enough. Report to me as soon as possible.

Kjelle felt cold terror drain the blood from his face. *Must I go to the top of the Silfjall for a ... a light?* With an effort, he managed to hide his panic. 'Immediately, Lord.' He saluted as the soldiers did, fist to the shoulder. Sick with fear, he ran from his father's room into the great hall. 'Muus. Where are you, misbegotten spawn of a pig?'

Creaking, the old beech parted from its roots. The earth trembled as the giant tree came down with a scatter of snow and broken branches. 'That's five.' Harald Enske lodged his ax into the stump. He wiped the sweat from his face. 'Enough for today.' The old karl looked around the group. 'Well done, men.' His eyes rested on one of the weary faces. 'You too, Muus. We'll make a real Nord of you, one of these days.' The freedmen grinned at the foreman's jest.

Muus forced a smile, but said nothing. As a slave since childhood, he'd often been the butt of crude jokes, and hard hands had taught him not to show offense. He was sixteen now, a man, and every remark strengthened his resolve to run. His mind wandered to the countless escape plans he'd made and rejected. To run was one thing, to run and stay alive was quite something else. Holder Alman would go to any lengths to recapture an escaped slave and Muus knew he looked nothing like a Nord. He'd once seen himself, reflected in a pool of water. He'd seen his thin, pale face, half hidden behind tangled black hair. It wasn't a Nord's face at all. Besides, he was too small. Nord's were half as much taller than he. Loki's Joking, even many of their children topped him with ease. Running was not an option. Therefore, he waited and nursed his longing. His head filled with fantasies, he walked into a tree and yelped.

'Ya dreamin', slave boy?' Red Orn, a warrior with a long, ruddy beard, grinned, his rotten teeth bare. 'Y'are a maid, then?' He licked his lips.

Muus' face flushed, and he blessed the Long Night that veiled his shame. For someone to call him a girl was naming him unmanly, a mortal insult. With another Nord, this would've been a fighting matter. However, he was only a thrall. He had no honor, and he couldn't defend himself.

Orn grinned and gave him a poke with his elbow, so that he almost tripped.

'Watch where you're goin', you,' said Harald Enske without looking.

Muus clenched his fists and hurried to the front. *Orn, that brainless grub.* What made it worse, the warrior was one of Kjelle's toadies. Holderling Kjelle, his master and owner.

'Muus.' Kjelle stormed out of the longhouse, red-faced with anger. 'Why didn't you come when I called? I'll teach you not to listen.' He raised his hand to strike, when the calm voice of Harald Enske made him pause.

'Your thrall was with the logging crew, Holderling,' said the foreman.

Kjelle cursed, but he couldn't say anything without losing face. In his agitation he had forgotten he'd sent his slave away with the men into the forest, to have him out of the way while he was bedding the girl. He balled his fist. 'You're late.'

'The supper bell hasn't rung yet,' said Harald. 'We've downed five trees. That takes time.'

Kjelle took a deep breath. Why must they always argue with him? No one took him seriously. And that treacherous slave with his underhand tricks... Damn, he'd teach him. He shook his fist in Muus' face. 'We're going up the mountain. Old Siga's got a bag with my stuff ready. Pick it up and come right back. We leave immediately.'

'It's near the evening meal,' said Harald. 'Like every man here, Muus worked hard today.'

'By Thor!' shouted Kjelle. 'Do what I say. Get those things, we leave now.' While Muus hurried inside, the Holderling looked around the group. 'Hagen comes. I need two more men.' He pointed to Orn. 'You.' The ruddy warrior grinned, as if he were proud to be chosen. Orn would support his decisions. Not like Hagen, his father's *experienced* man. His glance fell on Jal. A timid lad, but a good fighter. 'You too. Go get your gear.' Then he looked up to the blue light on the mountain. *It's alves.'* He shuddered. *Svartalves.* 'Thor's Hammer, why must I go? I am the Holderling.' He realized too late that he had spoken aloud. Luckily, only Harald Enske was still with him.

'You're the Holderling,' said the foreman softly. 'That brings responsibilities. The men expect a leader, Kjelle. A fearless captain.'

Kjelle bit his lip. Harald was a man with authority, not someone to antagonize. 'I know.' He looked again at the light on the mountain. The blue light seemed full of invisible dangers. Alves with wicked axes, like in the old tales. *I can't. What should I do?* The fear fed his anger. What's keeping that bastard Muus? He wanted to shout, to vent his rage, but he forced the feeling down. He was the Holderling.

'Snowshoes?' Siga stared at Muus. 'Are you going up the mountain? After a full day's work in the forest?' She shook her head. 'Well, you're out of luck, lad; I've only this pair left. They are a bit small, even for you. Here is the young lord's backpack. And then ...' She hesitated. 'There is something about that light on the mountain. Something I should remember. Last night I dreamed of ravens. Ravens over Eidungruve.' Her wrinkled face looked troubled as she looked at Muus. 'Then I saw you and Kjelle in the snow in a forest, alone. A man came, an old one-eye with a beard. It was an oppressive dream, full of anger. Kjelle and you ... You are not friends.'

The Wisewoman was one of the few people who treated him as a human being instead of a lowly thrall, so Muus wasn't afraid to look her in the eye. 'Lady, I'm his slave, he is the Holderling of Eidungruve. How can I be his friend?'

'Friendship between a Nord and his thrall is not uncommon.'

'Between me and Kjelle Almansen it is, Wisewoman. Too often I felt his hard fist; too often I swallowed his insults.'

Siga sighed. 'Kjelle is not his father. Everyone follows Holder Alman blindly, but his son has yet to prove his worth. He could make a good leader, if he had more confidence.' Again, she shook her head, and her long, gray braids danced. 'He needs your help.'

Muus lowered his eyes and remained silent.

All hesitation vanished from Siga's eyes. 'Wait.' She turned to a chest against the wall. Muus watched how she moved herb satchels and small woven caskets, strings of colorful beads, large feathers of a strange animal and other paraphernalia of her craft. Mysterious things that piqued Muus' curiosity. Siga was a Wisewoman, follower of Freya and a weaver of spells. *Seidr* magic was a woman's art; men shouldn't know too much about such things. He frowned, somehow that thought rang hollow.

Then Siga turned back and held her hand out to him. From her fingers dangled a tiny bone on a leather lace. 'Here, this is yours. You wore it when they brought you here. It has power, but no type that I recognize or can use. Put it on, quick; Kjelle is waiting. Remember my words.'

The little bone was dry and light in Muus' hand. There was a rune word on it, but it was a sign he couldn't read. 'What is it? A finger bone? What does it mean?'

'I don't know,' said Siga. 'It is a finger bone. A human bone and it must be very old. I do not now this rune; perhaps it is a power word. It is male magic; I cannot read that. You will have to find out by yourself.'

Male magic? Was there such a thing? With some trepidation, Muus put the finger bone around his neck. Nothing happened. He shrugged; of course it didn't work, he wasn't a Wiseman. Stifling a curse, he hung Kjelle's pack on his back and grabbed the snowshoes. The amulet had to wait, or Kjelle would burst a blood vessel. If only he did... With a curt 'thanks' to Siga, he hurried outside.

'Muus.' The arrogant voice of his lord cut through the silent mountain air. 'Hurry up, you lazybones.'

'Yes, master.' Muus moved his shoulders. The straps of the backpack cut into his meager shoulders and bit into his bone. The thick layer of snow on the trail numbed his toes and made him stumble. He hurried to keep up. Of course he was slow. He had rags for boots and the oldest, most worn snowshoes of all Eidungruve. A child's pair, too small for even his feet. Curse them to Helheim. How could they expect him to walk on these? With balled fists, he stared at the beautifully made snowshoes and the sturdy leather boots of Jal in front of him. Boots. That was a dream. Expensive boots were not for slaves. Holder Alman was a hard master. Hard for everyone: himself, his karls, his cattle, his thralls. For everyone except his son. Holderling Kjelle was a spoiled blowhard, afraid of his own shadow. One of Muus' snowshoes struck a rock and he almost fell. Red Orn laughed at his wild arm waving.

'The little man wants to fly,' said he with a dirty grin. 'Shall I help you, boy?' He shoved Muus, who ended up sprawled in the snow.

Kjelle snorted with rage. 'Use your eyes, stupid.'

Before Muus could move, Kjelle's hard hands pulled him to his feet and slapped him in the face. 'Now go.'

Muus tasted the blood dripping down his chin. He grabbed a handful of fresh snow from the ground and pressed it to his nose, while he hurried after the others.

Halfway up the mountain they paused. In the valley below Muus saw the longhouses and the silver mine of Eidungruve, contrasting with the dark blue of the Long Night. A door opened and warm light shone. Warmth, the thought brought tears to his eyes. A plume of smoke rose from the bake-house, conjuring up images of Siga's fresh bread and hot porridge. For a moment, Muus thought he could smell the food and his stomach cried out. That mangy mongrel Kjelle was so fanatical to prove himself to his father, that his thrall missed his meal. And for what? To disturb the spirits of the mountain? Unwise foolishness. Cold, hungry and spitting mad, Muus turned away from the view across the valley.

'Muus,' commanded Kjelle. 'Come here. I'm hungry. '

The young slave hurried to his master, who without a word began rummaging in the backpack.

'Ah,' said Kjelle pleased, pulling out a round loaf of bread and a piece of cheese wrapped in linen. Eagerly he set his teeth in the bread, while Muus, seething, repacked his ransacked bag.

When the Holderling had eaten his fill, he threw the last chunk of bread to Muus. 'Here, that puny body of yours doesn't need much.'

The youngest of the three karls, Jal of the Fine Boots, waited until Kjelle had turned his back and shoved a chunk of hard cheese in Muus' hands. 'Take it,' said he. 'I have enough.'

Muus brought his hand to his head in thanks, his heart filled with bitter resentment. Jal's well-intentioned gift hurt his pride as much as Kjelle's beatings. Just in time he stuffed the chunk into his mouth, because Kjelle gestured them back on the path. Muus started to walk again, his curses stifled by the cheese.

After a bend in the path, Hagen halted. He peered at the ground, uncertain like a hound that found a fresh bear track. 'Holderling, the snow - I don't trust it.'

Kjelle cast a suspicious glance at the ground. 'What about it?'

The karl hesitated. 'I don't know if it is safe to go further. The snow isn't solid. An avalanche ...'

'Nonsense,' said Kjelle, turning away. 'The slope looks fine. Keep moving; we're almost at the high pasture.'

The nearer they came to the plateau where in summer the sheep grazed, the brighter the blue glow became. The last stretch seemed like walking through the cold fires of Helheim, past rocks and snow, covered with dancing light. Muus glanced at Kjelle's face. He noticed the glistening sweat on Kjelle's forehead, the staring eyes and the hasty white puffs of his breathing. Muus knew Kjelle was scared. Muus remembered Kjelle's training sessions with Oskar, the drunken, blustering weapon master. Muus had been there, guarding the Holderling's weapons, watching his master fight, sweating and shaking, while Oskar shouted and pressed him. Kjelle was always angry after those sessions with Oskar, angry at his slave, never at the weapon master. Muus laughed soundlessly. Kjelle must be the only Nord who'd completed his manhood's Testing by hunting a nearly dead bear. Muus had been there. He'd carried his master's spears and he knew someone else had gone first and done the real work. It was because the Holderling's life was precious and he couldn't be risked, people said. Muus knew the truth. The Holderling with his blustery mouth and his hard hands was scared.

After three hours on the mountain, they reached the plateau where the sheep grazed in summertime.

'By Thor's Beard.' whispered Kjelle. In the middle of the field was a round hole, about a foot deep and round as the shield of a giant. The blue light radiated from the shield's center.

The men murmured uneasily. 'Alf work,' shouted Orn. 'We must get away from here, before the svartalves drag us into the mountain.' Muus saw his whole face contort in fear.'

'Svartalves are a bard's tale,' said Hagen. 'Shut up and wait for orders.' He looked at Kjelle.

The Holderling wiped the sweat from his face. 'Go see what it is,' said he, poking his slave.

Muus shrugged. The blue glow didn't scare him and he walked into the circle. The light enveloped him as if in welcome. In the middle lay a shard the color of a cloudless winter sky, translucent like a lump of ice and as big as the palm of his hand. This was where the glow came from. Without thinking, Muus picked up the shard. A noiseless flash covered him; a sharp pain came and went. As he stood there in a daze, staring at the glowing stone, Kjelle came up to him.

'What have you got there?' he snapped. 'Give it to me.' The Holderling held out a compelling hand.

Muus started to give him the stone, when a voice in his head said, 'No.'

'No?' said Kjelle in disbelieve.

With a shock, Muus realized that he had spoken aloud.

His master exploded in wrath. 'You mangy rat! Give it to me, or I'll leave your carcass here for the wolves.'

The skyshard strengthened Muus' resolve and he shook his head. 'It's mine,' said he in a soft voice. 'I found it.'

'You're a slave,' yelled Kjelle. 'Nothing is yours.' He grabbed Muus' hand and squeezed.

Muus tried to break free, but the Holderling was stronger. When Kjelle bent his middle finger back, he had to give in. He opened his hand and eagerly Kjelle grabbed the blue stone. The moment his fingers touched the shiny surface, a thunderclap echoed against the top of the Silfjall and shook the plateau. A massive tremor threw Kjelle and Muus hard against the mountainside. From somewhere came a cry of deadly fear, which was drowned out by a growling like the awakening of a large, hungry snow bear. Dazed, Muus saw an immense load of snow pass within an arm's length of where he lay. Without thinking, he pressed himself against the mountain, his ears filled with the wild roar of the avalanche. It happened in three or four heartbeats, before a final boulder bounced past and a swirling cloud of fine powder rose above the pasture. The roar died into deep silence.

It took a while before Muus found the courage to crawl out from under the narrow overhang that had saved his life. He stared in horror at the immense swath of bare rock the avalanche had left. No more snow, no more grass, the summer meadow had been ruined.

A sudden cramp penetrated through the shock and he looked at his hand. His fingers were stiff from holding on to the blue shard. All the light had gone; the stone lay cold and lifeless in his palm. He put it in the pouch around his neck. While he tried to stand, something clutched his ankles. Gazing down, he saw his old snowshoes, broken and useless. He cursed as he tore them from his feet, and walked to the edge of the precipice. Below him, the Hold, if there was anything left of it, lay hidden, unreachable behind a barrier of snow. Muus suppressed a scream and threw the snowshoes over the edge.

An immense calm came over him. This was it. There was no going back. The three Norns had cut his life thread; he'd die on this plateau. He turned around and saw Kjelle, curled up in the shadow of the overhang. A little further away lay Hagen, as a shapeless heap at the foot of the mountainside. Jal with his fine boots and Orn the Red Braggart had disappeared. Over the edge, probably.

He walked back to his master. Kjelle was unconscious; his face was deathly pale and a trickle of blood ran down from a gash in his forehead. Muus bent over him. He thought of all the times this coward had humiliated him and he felt his anger rise. His hand went for his knife, but with the blade half-drawn, he hesitated. *No. I can't just murder the bastard.* He resheated his knife and hurried over to Hagen. To his surprise, the karl still lived. There was blood in his beard and his legs lay folded in an odd angle under his body, but his eyes were alert.

'Well?' he asked when Muus knelt beside him.

The young slave shook his head. 'Everything is gone. I couldn't see Eidungruve and the path down has been obliterated. It's over, Hagen.'

'For me,' said the man. 'Not for you. Listen, there's a tunnel. A crack in the mountainside; it leads through the mountain. Old Garn fell down it. Took him all summer, but he came back. '

'Truly?' Muus knew his voice was hoarse. 'I thought it was just a tall story. Where is the tunnel?' His throat constricted by unexpected hope.

'Follow the mountain side. The Holder had large rocks placed around the hole to prevent the sheep from falling inside.'

'I'll find it. How are you? '

'Done for,' said the karl. 'Them snowshoes have broken me legs.' He growled. 'The damned things themselves are still intact. Where are Jal, Orn, and the Holderling? '

Muus gestured with his head. 'Jal and Orn have disappeared; the avalanche must have taken them. Kjelle is over there. He's unconscious, but alive.' Something of his disgust must have crept into his voice, for Hagen grimaced.

'Don't hurt him.' He balled a weak fist. 'I know how he treated you, it wasn't right. You're free now. Flee if you want, but let Kjelle live.'

Muus nodded. 'Don't worry, I will. I'm not dishonorable enough to kill an unconscious opponent.'

Hagen relaxed. 'Yes, I knew you were a good lad. Straight away I saw it when I bought you at that slave auction. You were the only child that didn't cry.'

'You bought me? Why?' Muus remembered a man, who took him away from the auction. His voice had sounded friendly, but he'd been as faceless as all other memories.

'Holder Alman instructed me to get a little boy as a thrall for Kjelle. He needed a companion. Friendships between master and slave aren't uncommon.'

'Ha!' Muus' laugh was bitter. 'Siga said the same - it must have been something you ate. Kjelle and I, friends? Not on this side of Godsdammer.'

'No, we saw that soon enough,' said Hagen with difficulty. 'Kjelle hated you from the moment he laid eyes on you. Don't know why. Only that he's ... not as brave as you.'

'Kjelle is a coward. Nobody knows that better than you, Kjelle's bear-killer.'

Hagen looked uncomfortable. 'So you know that. Look, Kjelle was the Holder's only child. Alman's wound... His terrible secret was the loss of his manhood's balls in that last battle. The Holder won't beget any more offspring. As a result he became overprotective of his son, turning the lad into a spoiled weakling.' He coughed and a trickle of blood leaked from his mouth. 'Broken ribs.' He coughed again, pressing his hand to his mouth. 'Alman repents his coddling. That's why he sent Kjelle up here.' The old karl looked at Muus. 'Bring the Holderling to me, will you? I've a request.'

The young slave nodded. 'I'll fetch him.'

Kjelle sat in the snow with his arms clasped around his legs. As Muus neared he looked up, his face wet with tears.

'Did you see it?' said Muus cruelly. 'Your Hold is gone. And your avalanche has wiped out the mountain path. We can't go back, Kjelle. We'll die here.'

His master didn't react. All his bluster had disappeared with the avalanche and naked distress stared from his eyes.

Muus snorted. 'Hagen's asking for you. His ribs and his legs are broken.'

Without a word, Kjelle came to his feet.

While Muus had gone for the Holderling, the wounded karl had wrestled himself out of his cloak and his heavy coat. 'What are you doing?'

'You take it,' said the karl. 'It's warm. Real snow wolf.' For a moment, his hand stroked the hair plumes along the seam. 'I killed him meself, when you were small.' Then he looked at Kjelle. 'Holderling, I'm of no more use - dead, but for the dying. Let me go like a warrior, by your hand, so that I can enter Valhalla.'

Kjelle's face was ashen. 'I ...' His hand went to his hunting knife and Muus saw how he trembled. The young lord put the tip of the knife into the spot under Hagen's sternum and froze. With eyes wide with horror, he stared at the precious steel.

Hagen looked at him and seemed to understand his fear. 'I'm your father's man, Kjelle. And you are your father's son. The warrior's death is my right and your duty, Kjelle Almansen.'

Kjelle hesitated. 'I can't.'

'Do it,' whispered Hagen. 'Spare me the suffering, Lord.'

Kjelle stared at the knife while the tears ran down his face.

'I can't. I ... '

'Ah, Kjelle, cowardly dog!' cried Muus. 'Here then, old Nord.' He brought his hand down on Kjelle's fist. The blade plunged deep into Hagen's chest. The karl jerked once, his life departing with the blood flowing from his mouth and it was over.

Kjelle stared at Hagen, at the knife and then at Muus. 'He's dead,' said he, and then, with a trace of his normal anger: 'Why did you do that?'

'Why didn't you?'

Kjelle grew red. 'You ... You ... ' Then his hands pounded Muus' face. Muus had expected something and rolled away. Kjelle dived after him, lashing out with his fist. Muus' head snapped back and he yelled. With Kjelle's fists beating his chest and shoulders, Muus' hands searched for something with which to strike the Holderling. *A stone.* he prayed. Instead, he found something metallic. The grip of a sword. Hagen's sword, which had escaped from its sheath during the karl's fall. Kjelle crouched over Muus, nose to nose, his hands around Muus' neck. The young slave fought for air. With his last strength, he hit Kjelle hard with the sword knob on his temple. Kjelle screamed. His grip slackened and Muus managed to push him away.

Muus came to his knees and placed the tip of the sword on Kjelle's throat. 'Are you done?' Splashes of blood from his chin dripped onto Kjelle's coat. 'Are you done or must I kill you?'

Kjelle stared at him with murder in his eyes, but then all the tension flowed out of him. His eyes filled with tears and he nodded. 'Was it true what you said?'

'That we can't go down? Yes, the avalanche swept away the last trees and wiped out the path. At the bottom, you'll see only snow and broken trunks. The Hold must be buried deep.'

'Let me get up,' said Kjelle without a trace of his earlier arrogance. 'I must see.'

Muus put the sword under his arm. 'Come.'

Near the edge of the plateau, Kjelle stopped and stared into the valley for a long time. 'You're right,' said he at last. 'We are cut off. It is our fate to die here.'

'We'll see,' said Muus. 'But first I must have other clothes. You're warmly dressed,' said he with a look at Kjelle's handsome coat. 'I'm not.'

'Of course not,' said Kjelle. 'My coat cost more than a new slave.'

Muus spat on the ground, but said he nothing. He knew that Kjelle was right. At Hagen's body, he began to untie the snowshoes from the dead man's broken feet. The boots of the old karl fit Muus over his own leg wraps and the heavy coat of snow wolf fur came to his knees. He buckled Hagen's sword belt over it and sheathed the weapon defiantly.

Kjelle's eyes followed his every move. 'Thralls aren't allowed to bear swords.'

Muus looked at him. 'I should've given it to you, I suppose? After you tried to strangle me? I'm not crazy, Kjelle.'

The young lord's face twitched. 'I'm your master.'

'No longer.' Muus grinned without a trace of humor. 'I'm a free man. And you can't prove I'm not.'

A spasm of anger passed over Kjelle's face. 'The word of the Holderling of Eidungruve against yours?'

Muus' grin became sharper. 'How can you prove that you are who you say you are, Holderling?'

Kjelle's eyes widened. 'But I ...' Muus waited with some malicious pleasure until Kjelle realize the truth. He wasn't presented yet, no one outside of Eidungruve knew him. Without a headman at his side, without the sword of his father in his hand, without money and fine clothes, Kjelle was nobody. Then his broad shoulders sank and his clenched fists relaxed. 'I see it now.'

Muus looked at Kjelle's face and recognized the mix of shock, fear, and the strange helplessness that so often preceded one of his rages. But not this time.

'I must go down,' said Kjelle after a while. 'I must know if Eidungruve still exists.'

Muus was silent for a moment. *And I? Do I go with him? Now is my chance to run. Only... where will I go?* He felt heat on his chest and without thinking his hand went to the stone under his tunic. It radiated warmth and as he put his hand over the pouch, it seemed the semi-darkness of the Long Night faded. A landscape of red rocks under a broiling sun appeared before his eyes. With a surprised yelp he pulled his hand back. The hot vision dissolved into the cold present. He blinked. *Was that a dream? I felt the heat on my skin.* He saw Kjelle staring at him, with a lost look in his eyes. Muus rubbed his face. *I can't trust him.* But he knew he couldn't run and let the oaf fend for himself. Not here on the mountain.

'What will you do with Hagen? We can't bury him here and most stones went down with the avalanche. Still, you don't want him to go walking as a draug.'

Kjelle froze. 'By Thor, no.' He went over to the dead karl. After a moment's hesitation, he closed the staring eyes and straightened the body in the snow. 'I'll come back for you, Hagen.' His voice trembled. 'Sleep, brave Nord, you don't have to walk. You will receive an honorable burial. I, Kjelle Almansen, so swear.' Then he straightened his back. 'Let's go.'

'Aren't you forgetting anything?'

'What?'

Muus gestured around. 'There's no way down.'

'If we stay here, we'll die,' said Kjelle with despair in his voice. 'We have to get down.'

Muus nodded. 'Sure. But not along the vanished path.' He nodded to the heavy backpack. 'Your turn to wear it.'

Kjelle opened his mouth and closed it again. Without a word, he hung the pack on his back.

The two walked along the side of the mountain until Muus saw the spot Hagen had described.. There was a dark opening in the base of the rock wall, with large stones around it. 'There's our way out.'

'A hole in the mountain?' Kjelle's voice rose. 'That's svartalf work.'

Muus shrugged. 'Perhaps. According to Hagen it is a tunnel.' His smile was grim. 'Old Garn's Tunnel.'

Kjelle howled like a wolf with his paw in a trap. 'Garn. He had to defeat hundreds of monsters before he passed through the mountain.'

'Old Garn was a great storyteller,' said Muus. 'Hearing him, he'd been eaten a dozen times. Listen, Holderling, we've no choice. We can't stay here. Down the slope is suicide. Through the tunnel we may have a chance. And if not, you can show me how bravely a Nord dies.'

The scornful undertone in Muus' words had effect, for with a cry of despair, Kjelle leapt into the hole.

CHAPTER 2 - OLD GARN'S TUNNEL

Muus jumped after him. The hole was deeper than he had expected. A smooth tunnel of ice, which carried them diagonally down through the dark. Someone screamed and he wasn't sure if it was Kjelle, or himself. After an endless time came a sharp left turn and then they plunged into nothingness. It was not deep, where they fell, six feet at most, and they ended up in a painful heap of arms and legs on a rocky surface.

'Muus.'

'Get your fingers out of my face, you cack-handed clod,' cried Muus and his voice echoed in the cave: lod... lod... lod...

'I can't see.' Kjelle almost screamed. 'We're dead.'

'Shut up.' Muus kicked in Kjelle's direction. He felt his foot make contact and the wailing broke off. 'Be still and let me think.' He stood up and tried to orient himself. The darkness was oppressive in its intensity. Around him was the mountain. All that rock over his head, how could such a tunnel exist without collapsing? He heard something shifting somewhere and his heart began to pound.

Beside him, Kjelle's sob broke the tension. The Holderling's fear stank of sweat. 'Where is Sun?'

'Huh?' Muus looked in the direction of Kjelle's voice, but in the absolute dark not even a silhouette was visible.

'In the Long Night, she hides in the earth,' said the young lord absently. 'But where then is her light?'

Muus sniffed. 'The earth is large. She could be anywhere.' He thought a moment. 'Besides, that chariot of hers wouldn't fit into this tunnel. The svartalves will have built a beautiful hall for it somewhere.'

There was silence.

'Muus, Godsdammer. You give light.' Kjelle's voice was high and breathless, as if he was only just skirting hysteria.

Yet he was right. Muus saw a faint blue glow grow around him. The stone on his chest felt warm, as warm as when he had picked it up on the pasture. He opened the pouch around his neck and squinted against the blue glow that radiated out. 'It's not me. It is the stone. '

'What!' Kjelle's voice echoed against the walls. 'Have you brought that damned thing? Thor! That stone is the cause of everything. Throw it away.'

'Nonsense,' said Muus. 'You didn't have to touch it. The stone is mine. When I hold it, nothing happens.'

'It's dangerous.'

'And it lights our way, so we can see where we're walking. Well, shall we go or is there something you must do here?'

Kjelle brought his head close to that of Muus. In the stone's light, his face contorted with rage. He waved white-knuckled fists under Muus' nose. 'You ... you ...'

The young slave braced himself, but it wasn't necessary. Kjelle's facial muscles slacked, the fire in his eyes died and his shoulders slumped. He gave a dull nod. 'We go.'

With a slight shiver, Muus walked on. The tunnel walls around them were smooth and dripping with moisture. The blue glow of the stone reflected in drops and puddles, so they seemed to move along the bottom of a river. Stone teeth grew up and down and everywhere was the sound of water.

'Why?' said Kjelle after a long silence. His voice was flat, emotionless.

Muus did not have to ask what he meant. 'What do you think? Because you're the stupid son of a drunken duck, perhaps?'

Kjelle stopped and peered sideways at Muus. 'How could I know that a small stone like that would cause an avalanche?'

Muus blew his nose in his fingers. 'You couldn't. You should've kept your greedy paws to yourself.' He muttered a curse when a cold trickle landed between his eyes. 'You Nords always want to have everything. Stinking thieves you are, every one of you.' He thought of the round huts of his village. *Murderers and abductors of children.* A choking sound made him look aside. Kjelle's face, deadly blue in the light of the stone, was twisted with fear and anger battling in him for dominance.

'I'm your master. You should have obeyed.'

'The stone didn't think so. He rejected you, Nord.'

'But why? Who sent that stone? The svartalves? They hate us, they're deceitful creatures.'

Muus shrugged. 'I don't know anything about svartalves.'

'You look like them, slave.' Kjelle's voice was vicious. 'Small, black haired and mean.'

'I should've left you on the plateau, stupid Nord,' said Muus unperturbed. He was amazed that Kjelle's words didn't touch him anymore. 'Maybe your Gods would've saved you.' He looked at Kjelle. 'Probably not. You're not man enough for them, Kjelle Almansen.' After this insult, he moved his hand toward the grip of his sword, but it wasn't necessary. Kjelle only shook his head, too deep in his misery to be angry.

'Why did that stone come? To punish me? To ... to test me? A test ... and I failed.'

'By the Gods, man, do you really think a stone falls from the sky to test you? Are you that important? Don't be daft. You wanted something that wasn't meant for you. Because of your stupidity, many people died. That's your fault. What will you do now?' The fear in Kjelle's face was so great that Muus looked away. 'Let's go. Talking won't solve anything. The answer lies with the Gods. Yours or mine.'

The loud sound around them was their breathing, pierced by the plink, plink of the droplets that escaped from the rock over their heads. The thin layer of water on the floor of the tunnel muffled their footsteps and there was near-complete silence.

'Your Gods?' said Kjelle after a while. 'Who are they?'

'I ... do not know.' Muus recalled the images from his dreams; the round huts on the riverbank and the faceless people. 'My memories begin when I arrived at Eidungruve. Hagen brought me. He had a gray horse, and he talked to me. I couldn't understand him, but his voice sounded ... not threatening. Funny, I remember all that so well. But who my parents were? No idea. Nor do I care, that's all gone now. The Hold was my home, even though I hated it.' Again, there was silence.

'I hated you from the moment you arrived,' said Kjelle from the twilight. 'Your pose, your pride; the way you looked at me. You, my own slave, laughed at me. Always you worked against me, made me look ridiculous. Me, the Holderling. With your hypocritical politeness: yes, master; no, master, and you laughing behind my back. I should have beaten you to death.'

'You've beaten me enough.'

'Not enough,' said Kjelle in a near-whisper. 'You're still alive.'

Muus shook his head. 'If you didn't want me, why I had to accompany you everywhere?'

'You had to. I ...' Kjelle fell silent.

All at once, it dawned on Muus. 'You needed me to feel brave.'

'Shut up,' said Kjelle in a tone that sent Muus for his sword. The sound of the blade along the sheath had them both stepping backward. Without speaking, they went forward.

The dark path made Muus imagine rows of alves with pickaxes, tunneling through the rock. Skinny black creatures, ugly and crooked by their life underground. He shuddered. As in a bad dream, he walked on.

A ripping sound followed by a shrill scream shocked Muus out of his thoughts. He looked up just in time to see his companion disappear into the ground. Somehow, a crack had opened in the floor beneath his feet and swallowed him.

On his knees, Muus crawled towards the edge of crevice. The screaming and sobbing told him Kjelle was still alive. 'You're all right?'

A stream of unintelligible words answered him. The young Nord was stuck some six feet below him. Wild-eyed, he looked up at Muus. 'Get me out of here.'

'Easy now, breathe deeply. Recount the names of all your ancestors.'

'My ancestors? Kjelle, son of Alman, son of Hralf, son of Rognar... Argh, what's that for?'

'It helps you not to panic,' said Muus calmly. 'Can you stand?'

Kjelle shook his head. 'Bottom's too narrow.'

Muus lay flat on his belly and reached down with Hagen's sword. Hang the bag on the cross-guard.' Hand over hand he pulled the weapon back up, until he could swing the backpack down beside him. 'Well,' said he. 'At least we've got that.'

'You're not leaving me?'

Muus said nothing. A voice inside him whispered, *This is your chance. Let him rot.* He pulled off his coat, Hagen's heavy snow wolf coat. From sleeve to sleeve, it would be just long enough.

'Muus!' Panic rang in Kjelle's voice. 'Are you there?'

'Sure,' said Muus curtly. 'I wouldn't kill you this way.'

A second sound of tearing rock rent the air and Kjelle screamed. 'I can't hold on!'

'Quickly,' Muus hung the coat over the edge and grabbed one of the sleeves with both hands, while he gripped a nearby dripstone with his legs. 'Try to climb up; I can't pull you out on my own. And make sure you don't tear my coat or I will murder you.'

Gibbering with fear, Kjelle worked his way up. The rough wall of the crevasse scraped the skin from his hands and knees, while a sweating Muus pulled his coat up hand over hand. At last, Kjelle managed to place his elbows on the edge. Muus grabbed the back of Kjelle's waistband and with their combined strength the Holderling heaved himself back onto the floor of the tunnel.

Kjelle looked at Muus without speaking. His bloodied face was twisted in a mask of horror so intense that Muus got goose bumps. 'Let's get away from here.'

Quivering all over, the Holderling picked up the backpack.

They walked for another hour, when Kjelle abruptly stopped. 'I can't go on,' said he, with tears streaming down his face.

Muus sighed. He'd been working hard all day, logging trees. After that, he had to climb that bleeding mountain path and now this tunnel. He was tired, but he could've kept walking. He wanted to be free of this tunnel more than anything, but it was clear Kjelle was suffering from shock. 'Let's try to sleep,' said Muus, nodding to one of the many nooks in the rock wall.

Moving like a draug, Kjelle stumbled to the small recess and dropped. Muus sat beside him, listening to the snores of his companion. *Gods, I wanted to escape Eidungruve. But did it have to be this way?* Then he curled up against Kjelle and, back to back, they slept.

After an indeterminate amount of time, Muus woke, cold and hungry. Kjelle sat staring at him; his face a death mask and his movements stiff.

'Ready to go?' asked Muus.

Without a word, Kjelle rose and started to walk. They went on down the tunnel towards whatever might wait for them at the end. Time passed immeasurable in that tunnel. How long had they walked? Hours? A day? More?

Suddenly Kjelle spoke. 'It is getting colder.'

Muus looked up. The moisture on the tunnel wall was frozen and icicles had taken the place of the stone dragon's teeth.

'Light!' In a feverish excitement, the Holderling hurried forward. Far away was a narrow strip of what looked like daylight. He started to run.

'Watch out,' said Muus. 'It's ...' but it was too late. A thin layer of ice had formed on the ground and Kjelle crashed down. '... slippery.'

Kjelle stared at him, livid. Then he rose and went on slowly to the beckoning light.

Here, the tunnel ended. The opening they had hoped for proved to be a fissure in the rock through which a pale glimmer shone.

'O cursed Loki's Trick, it's frozen shut.' Kjelle pounded his fist on the ice, through which the treacherous light from the outside world beckoned them. 'Rock solid,' said he with tears in his eyes.

'We have knives,' said Muus. 'We can hack a way out.'

Kjelle licked his bleeding lip and nodded. He crouched down at the fissure with his hunting knife and started on the ice. The layer was thick, the two young men tired and cold. They had to take turns working, so it was a long time before their bleeding hands had hacked away enough ice to wriggle through the opening. For once Muus was thankful for his small stature, as he slipped like a small, black-haired, fox through the hole. Kjelle's massive form couldn't follow, however much he squirmed and groaned.

'Take off your clothes,' said Muus. 'They make you fat.'

Kjelle snarled something that was unintelligible, but he obeyed. Naked, he managed to squeeze himself through the opening. 'Is this the other end of the tunnel?' said he, as he put his shirt and his hairy coat back on over the bloody scratches on his body.

Muus looked around. 'We're in an ice cave,' said he. 'There won't be any ice inside a mountain. This must be the glacier from Garn's tales. Maybe he wasn't such a fantast after all.'

'Then we're nearly out of here?'

Muus grimaced. 'I hope so. At least there weren't any monsters.' He stepped forward. 'There's an opening.' A narrow corridor led to a second, smaller space.

'Wait,' said Kjelle and his voice trembled. The second cave was littered with gnawed remains of animals, most of them frozen. 'Those dead rabbits are still fresh.'

Then they saw a triangular head with two wide-open eyes staring at them. 'Snow wolf.' whispered Kjelle.

'Freya's Blood.' Without hesitation, Muus drew his sword. He knew which end was up, that was about all.

Kjelle looked at him, deadly pale. 'What now?' His lips quivered. At that moment the wolf sprang.

Muus yelled. The snow wolf hesitated in midair and that broke his pounce. Reflexively the young slave struck and he felt the sword slide deep under the animal's ribs. Man and beast fell and a puddle of blood formed on the icy soil. The smell of wet dog filled Muus' nostrils. He pushed against the hairy corpse. 'It didn't touch me. Thank the Gods.' He stood up and pulled his sword from the body of the beast.

'It's dead.' Kjelle looked bewildered from the dead wolf to Muus. 'It's really dead.'

'They won't come deader,' said Muus with a grimace of pure relief. Then he stooped and cut off the wolf's silver-white tail. For a moment, he stood with it in his hands, and then he pulled it through the belt around his waist. 'My thanks to you, Fenrisson Snow Wolf, for your gift.'

On Kjelle's face, disbelief and anger fought for supremacy. 'I didn't know you could handle a sword.'

Muus shrugged. 'Let's go.'

'We need food,' said Kjelle.

'Snow wolf?' Muus' gaze went to the dead wolf. It looked tough.

The Holderling stared at him. 'You're no hunter. Wolves are carnivores; their meat won't feed us. Deer, rabbit, everything that lives off plants and roots is edible.'

'I'm not a hunter,' admitted Muus. 'Give a thrall a bow and arrow? Your father wouldn't dare.' He walked to the exit of the cave. 'Let's find a rabbit. It's your turn to kill a monster, Holderling.'

Kjelle grimaced, but said he nothing.

The crack in the ice was about ten yards long, but only snow wolf-wide and Kjelle took off his clothes again. Wriggling and cursing mightily, he too came through and side by side, they stood in the familiar semi-darkness of the Long Night.

Kjelle, oblivious to the snowflakes collecting on his bare chest, looked around. Nearby, a dark river ran past, against a backdrop of woodlands. 'The Jerna.' His voice was full of disbelief. 'We made it.'

Muus nodded. *Freedom at last.* He wanted to laugh, cry, but all at once he was too tired.

Hunger forced them into action. Moon's cart drove across the sky, as it had the night of the avalanche, so at least one day and one night must have passed. Strangely, Muus wasn't tired anymore, but his stomach growled like a barn full of slop-starved pigs. His mouth was dry and he let a small handful of fresh snow melt on his tongue. The path through the mountain had dripped of water, but that was almost liquid stone, undrinkable. With his thirst quenched, he looked around. Behind them rose a glittering wall, like a river of ice cut off by a giant saw. *Did we come through that?* He whistled. *A story for by the hearth. With a lot of fantasy for the details.* He sighed. 'Should we go to the left or to the right?'

Kjelle's forehead wrinkled. 'To the right. Garn said that when he left the tunnel he followed Sun's chariot.' He nodded toward Moon above them. 'Like he does.'

They walked on until they reached a bend in the river.

'There is a fjord,' said Kjelle and he pointed with his head. A row of stones formed a natural way to the other side of the fast-flowing river.

On the last stone Muus froze. 'Stand still.' He sank to his knees and put his hand into the water. Carefully, his fingers approached the underside of the trout that he saw. The fish hung motionless in the water against the tide, resting from the upstream journey. Muus stroked the belly of the fish until it fell into a trance. Then he seized the trout with his hands and threw it onto the ground, to end its voyage with a fist-sized stone.

Open-mouthed Kjelle looked at him. 'How did you do that?' Then, with horror, 'Magic?'

Muus bared his teeth. 'It's an old fisherman's trick. Petting it makes the trout go to sleep and wham, you have it. Can you make a fire? '

'Y.yes,' said Kjelle. 'But I'm not good at it.'

'Then start practicing.' Muus turned back to the water. 'I'll need an hour at least.' *I learned trout tickling as a child. Why do I remember that now?*

Kjelle's campfire wasn't much, and the fish was only half-cooked, but it was food and they were hungry. Then they dug a hole in the snow, curled up and slept.

That night Muus dreamt of burning lands, and a standing stone in a fiery cave. It was hot there, boiling hot. But when he woke up hours later, everything about him was cold and he had to piss. When he finished, he sought some dry wood and started a new fire.

It was quiet in the forest. Moon's cart had already gone from the sky. Daybreak. Unexpected tears stung Muus' eyes. He should now be feeding the pigs, he thought, while Siga and her women were preparing the morning meal. Siga... He froze. The Wisewoman had told him her dream of ravens above Eidungruve. Odin's ravens were sacred; harbingers of battle. Their presence where they did not belong was a sign of war. She had seen him and Kjelle alone in a snowy forest. A true vision, for here they were, and there lay plenty of snow. Siga's dream didn't bode well for Eidungruve.

Muus stood up and walked to the banks of the Jerna. He scooped up a handful of icy water and let it warm up in his mouth before he swallowed. Bending over, he scanned the surface for trout. Only half of his mind was on the fishes, the fate of Eidungruve and its people bothered him more than he cared to admit. This was his eleventh winter in the Hold. He'd grown up here and despite everything, it had become his home; the only family he had. Without thinking he caught one trout after another, until six laid in a row on the bank. His mind wandered to the past. The faceless people from his dreams. Who were they? For the first time he felt a trace of curiosity. Where did he come from? Not from the Norden; not with hair as black as his, or a skin so pale. White as a snow mouse. Everyone called him Muus, but it wasn't his name. He didn't know his name.

Hurriedly he gathered his six fish and went back to the fire. When he got there, he almost dropped his catch. An old man in a gray cloak sat by the fire, the flames staining his white beard red. On his knees, he had a long walking stick. Kjelle sat opposite him, his eyes wide and staring. When Muus approached, the old one turned his face in his direction. He was missing one eye. 'Six trout. Do you eat with us, stranger? '

The old man laughed. 'How courteous. But no, I must decline.' He paused, cocking his head. 'You won't have any wine?'

Muus spread his hands. 'We have what we can catch.'

'I was afraid of that. Don't give it a thought.' His one eye twinkled. 'Tell me, why are a young Nord and Bryt wandering through the frozen forests of Dalland? There must be a saga behind it, worthy of the best skalds.'

Muus thought for a moment and the old man's smile grew. 'Caution is wisdom, for all you know I am that rascal Loki in disguise.'

The young man nodded. 'I don't doubt your sincerity.' He glanced sideways at Kjelle but the Holderling stared wordlessly at their visitor. Muus sat down by the fire and rubbed his stiffened hands, while he spoke of the stone, the avalanche and their journey through the mountain.

The old man followed his story with rapt attention. When Muus finished, he smiled. 'So you're the Shardheld. The skyshard makes a strange choice. May I see him?'

With care, Muus took the stone out of its pouch around his neck. The blue shard shone in the palm of his hand.

'Avalanche Maker,' said the old man as if greeting an acquaintance. Then he looked at Muus. 'The skyshard bears many names and none of them flattering. This one is new. He is a merciless burden, Shardheld, while your strength is limited. Follow the river into the forest. One rest down river you will find Belisheim, a house of study wisdom and magic. Tell the Völva your story. Say that Harbard sent you.' He stood up and shook the folds of his cloak loose. 'I must go.'

'What is a skyshard?' asked Muus.

The old man gave him a sharp look. 'A piece of the sky.' He bowed. 'I wish you strength, Shardheld.' And with a glance at the still staring Kjelle, 'You as well, Holderling of Eidungruve.' Then he walked off into the woods, and disappeared amongst the trees.

'You're making an impression,' said Muus, while he opened the first trout with a flourish. 'You were staring at that old one as if you'd never seen a man before.'

'That was Odin, witless Bryt. Odin, the All-Father. '

Muus put his knife down. 'Odin? Why? Because he'd lost an eye? He said that he was called Harbard.'

'I knew it when I saw him. Harbard? That's one of Odin's names.'

Muus shrugged and went back to his fish. He had more important things on his mind than Nordish superstition. 'What's a Bryt?'

Kjelle's mouth fell open. 'You don't know? I never realized, but that's you, a wildman from Brytanna, where the barbarians live.' Something like contempt entered his voice. 'Small as children are the Bryts, with an ugly, dirty skin and they are bone thin. Like the svartalves.' He ducked just in time to avoid a trout that Muus had thrown. 'That's what the bards say.'

'Clean your own fish, you blond half-troll,' growled Muus. 'Or let those bards do it for you. This wildman has worked enough for the morning.'

While Kjelle picked clumsily at the slippery entrails of his trout, Muus stared into the fire. *Brytanna. Where the barbarians live.*

'Muus?'

'What?' His name recalled him from the labyrinth of his thoughts.

'It's snowing.' Kjelle threw the bones of the last trout in the bushes and sighed. 'We'd better go.'

Muus nodded and began to pull the fire apart with a stick. Moments later, they walked away along the river, into the forest.

CHAPTER 3 – MESSENGER

Tuuri led his horse down the ship's gangway in a state of happy anticipation. *Sleep on, good people; here comes the herald of change.* His hand touched the pieces of parchment inside his tunic. Here were the orders that would set Jarl Rannar's great plan into motion.

He paused on the small wooden strip that served as a quay and looked around. *So this is Helmshaven. It doesn't look much.* Compared to Westhal, his lord's town, this northernmost harbor was a collection of hovels. Little houses, looking as if they had been cobbled together from driftwood, with thatched roofs covered in gull shit. *At least the chickens were inside in this weather.* Not the pigs, though, and Tuuri waited impatiently while a fat sow moved aside to let him pass.

It started to snow, the flakes drowning in the slush that covered the streets. He walked his horse out of town, careful to avoid the largest mud puddles. The guard at the gate gave him a cursory glance, his attention on the pieces of wood he was feeding to his little brazier. Tuuri raised his hand in greeting, mounted and went into the forest, whistling.

Tuuri was well satisfied with life. He was a Jarl's messenger at eighteen, with a whole future of great deeds before him. A future befitting one who was a Fynni on his father's side. His gloved fingers touched the engraved sky symbol on his left cheek. It was a tribal mark his father had given him on his eighth name day and he wore it with pride. Fynni were the original people of the Ostmark, living there long before the Nords came. They were a nation of tribes, ruled by powerful Tarkynni, leading in work and war, and the sa'amans talking to the Gods. Tuuri was proud to be part of that ancient people.

He smiled. The orders he carried were meant for a man of his kin. The Tarkynn of a Fynni warband. "Don't look for him, he'll find you," the Jarl said. Tuuri sighed. He knew all the stories told of Fynni deeds, and he longed for the chance to meet them, to be acknowledged as kin.

The snowfall thickened, soft flakes covering his wolf skin coat with a white layer. Tuuri shook them out of his dark curls, before pulling his hood over his head. The weather brought memories of his life in the Ostmark, where the snow never stopped falling, a land where the rivers were near permanently frozen and only the hardiest survived childhood. There he was born, to go where others would falter.

His horse's tenseness warned him at the same moment his ears caught the faint crackling in the frozen underbrush. *Wolves.* Tuuri grinned. *Poor beasts, they are in for a surprise.* He raised his hands and sang the ancient bonding words his father taught him. For a moment, all was still. The wolves had stopped and stared at him. Tuuri saw their ribs through their shaggy pelts. Something shimmered on the path and a bear appeared, large as the rider and his horse. It gave Tuuri a dirty glance, irritated by his summons.

My pardon for summoning you, Sha'akaii my friend. I am in need of your great strength. His totem bear growled and moved towards the wolves. Their pack leader howled in frustration. Silent as they'd come, the beasts disappeared into the dark. Tuuri let out a deep sigh.

Sha'akaii gave the young man a chilling look. *Be more careful next time.* With a speed unbelievable for something so large, he chased after the wolves.

Have a nice hunt, my friend, thought Tuuri as he set his horse to walking.

Hours later, even his sturdy horse started to tire. Her pace slowed to a crawl and her head hung low in exaggerated weariness. 'Yes, I know,' said Tuuri with a grin. 'I'll find us a nice place to sleep.' At a spot were the snow had piled high, he halted. He fed his horse some grain and took a bite of bread and cheese from his saddlebags. Whistling softly, he dug himself a shallow hole in the snow, pulled his cloak around him and went to sleep.

A sharp kick in the ribs awakened him. Tuuri tensed, dagger in hand, and stared up at the young man before him. 'Fynni,' said he, recognizing the other's face markings on both cheeks. 'You shocked me out of my skin.'

The other laughed. 'You frighten easily, Fynnikin.'

That sounded like an insult.

Tuuri rose and put away his knife. 'I expected you, only not in the middle of the night.'

The young man showed his teeth. It wasn't a smile. 'I expected you awake, not sleeping.'

Tuuri frowned at the hostility in his voice. 'How are you named, brother?'

The young man stared at him, his thin face twisted into a sneer. 'I'll tell you once, Fynnikin. I am Vulf, Tarkynn of the Yenchinnii. I am no brother of yours.'

Tuuri felt the blood drain from his face. His throat constricted and he swallowed. 'I... I am Tuuri Little Dagger, Jarl Rannar's messenger.' He squared his shoulders. 'I carry orders for you.'

Vulf turned his head away. 'Later. We're on a raid. Join us.' His face was bleak. 'It'll show you our Fynni ways.'

Tuuri knew it wasn't a request. He rose, shook the snow from his cloak and went to get his horse. The enormity of Vulf's rejection had made Tuuri numb. Shame clutched at his heart and he felt like weeping. With difficulty, he kept his voice under control. 'What kind of a raid? I'm not heavily armed.'

'Don't be afraid,' said Vulf 'It's punishment against a spy's family. There's no danger involved, Fynnikin.'

Tuuri bit his lip. That wasn't what he'd meant. 'Lead the way, Tarkynn.'

Vulf's men formed a solid block of warriors, twenty-five strong. Ulvhednar, he saw by their badges, the most fanatical of all Fynni warriors, who lived and died at the word of their chief. He didn't like their faces. They seemed empty, devoid of any humanity. 'Is this your whole force?'

Vulf stared at him, his eyes like stones. 'No.' He looked away and Tuuri shivered.

They followed the road till they came to an intersection, where they turned right. It led to a small house overlooking the sea. With a wave of his hand, Vulf sent his men into position. 'Come,' said he, and with five men at their back, they walked to the front of the house.

Before Vulf could lay his hand on the handle, someone opened the door and a man's voice said, 'Who's there?' The man must have seen the warriors, for he tried to close the door. Vulf threw himself forward and they stormed inside. The man at the door slammed against the right wall. His nose started to bleed.

Tuuri looked around. To his left a dark-haired woman covered a scream with her hands. A young man of his own age had pushed a little boy behind him. They were small people. The man with the bleeding nose came barely to Tuuri's shoulder, and he wasn't tall.

'You have a nice house,' said Vulf conversationally. 'Nice view, comfortable. A pretty woman, as well. You've got it made, haven't you?'

The small man wiped his face. 'Tarkynn, your face markings show you're of the Fynni. Why do you come here? Why threaten us? Depart with your ulvhednar, go back to your mountains and leave us in peace.'

Vulf slapped him. 'You dirty svartalves. You're spies.' Over his shoulder he snarled, 'Kill them.'

His men drew their swords. The woman screamed once and died gurgling, slipping to the ground with a Fynni blade between her ribs. Her blood colored the rushes on the floor red. The youth crouched with a knife in his hands, waving it to and fro with desperate concentration. An ulvhednar laughed, moved his sword through the youth's guard and struck. While the young man sagged, his throat a gaping hole, the same warrior hit the little one with the flat of his sword above the ear. Near the door, the small man died last, cursing and shouting, pierced by three blades.

Tuuri stood there, watching the butchery with uncomprehending horror. This wasn't Rannar's glorious fight. This was murder. He walked over to the two boys. The eldest lay spread-eagled on top, his eyes empty. Underneath, the youngest lay, covered in blood, eyes half closed and his breath shallow. Tuuri turned around. 'These two are dead, Tarkynn,' said he, keeping his voice even.

Vulf bared his teeth. 'Are they now?' To the nearest man said he, 'Torch the house. Burn it all.'

They stepped outside. Vulf looked at Tuuri. 'The young one lived. I saw his eyelids flutter. No matter, he will die in the fire. You're a weakling, Fynnikin.'

'This is not Jarl Rannar's way, Tarkynn,' said Tuuri, his blood boiling.

Vulf gave him a contemptuous glance. 'We're Fynni. This is *our* way, Fynnikin. That's not something an Ostmark sheep like you would understand. You're no true-blood, let alone kin. Now give me your orders.'

Tuuri handed him the piece of parchment.

The Tarkynn glanced over the runes. 'Capture a silvermine, eh. Great, we'll do that.' Then he crumpled the message and threw it into the burning house. 'We're finished. Get out of my sight, Fynnikin.'

Tuuri looked around at the cruel, painted faces of the warriors around him, at the wolf head insignias on their tunics and the long, sharpened swords at their side. These were the fabled Fynni. The glorious berserkers of his race. His kin. His heart was sick as he rode away into the forest.

CHAPTER 4 - BELISHEIM

'It's about one rest to Belisheim,' the old man had said. One rest, a two-hour walk. Only not in a blizzard, with visibility less than the length of your little finger and every step a move in a wrestling match. Muus knew they couldn't seek the relative protection of the forest, for they had to stay close to the river. The Jerna River was their guide, without which they would be lost. When exhaustion forced them to stop, they dug a hole in the snow. There they slept, wrapped in their cloaks, huddled together. Hours later, they woke up, ate one of the leftover grilled trout from the day before and went on. The blizzard had stopped and the air spirits were celebrating its passing, for all around the sky played the bright green lights of their feasting. The two wanderers were too tired to speak, too miserable to quarrel as they trudged onward.

'There.' Kjelle pointed into the distance, and they could see torches burning through the trees and the outline of a palisade.

'Careful.' Muus' throat was hoarse, and he rubbed the freezing snow from his eyelashes. 'Let's see where we are before running inside.'

'Wisely spoken.' A muffled voice came out of the dark, deep and melodious. The torchlight danced on the shoulder of a cloaked figure. 'Two young men in the snow. Who are you and what do you seek in Belisheim?'

Kjelle stepped forward, hand raised. 'Greetings. We are victims of disaster, seeking shelter and food. Kjelle Almansen, I am, and my s... companion's name is Muus.'

'Welcome to Belisheim, Kjelle Almansen and Muus. Follow me; inside there is warmth, food, and drink.' They followed their escort inside the palisade, where Muus slowed down and looked around. A large house with several outbuildings. Good, solid woodwork, richly decorated with powerful characters that he couldn't read. 'There's no gate? Everyone and everything can walk inside?'

'We have neither gates nor guards,' said the escort. 'Belisheim is protected by the power of the Völva.' The door to the longhouse swung open. A wave of heat carried the smell of food to them. Muus' eyes began to water. *Fresh bread and stew.* Blinking, he looked around the common hall. Green branches and patches of holly reminded him it was Yuletide. They should've been celebrating now, even the thralls. A rough curse made him stare at the warriors lounging around a fire in the middle of the hall. They wore uniforms and their leather helmets had a metal wolf's head above the eyes. *Ulvhednar.* Only the mightiest in the kingdom were able to afford these berserkers. They kept their helmets and axes within reach, and their brutal faces, covered with strange tribal markings, saw red from the mead they had already enjoyed. One of them had jumped to his feet, a pockmarked fellow with a wolf's head as a cap and its dark gray pelt hanging down over the shoulders.

'You there,' he roared to their escort. 'We've been waiting a half-day already. When will the old woman see us? Jarl Rannar will not be pleased that his man Swinne was kept dangling.'

The hooded one moved a hand. 'Jarl Rannar's man Swinne will have to be patient. The auspicious moment for an audience has not yet arrived. Once the moment is there, the lady will have you summoned. Until then the food and drinks are at your disposal.'

The man cursed and sat down again. His hard eyes stared at Muus and Kjelle, while his lips twisted in a sarcastic grin. 'The lady does have time for two beardless wonders?'

'Fate leads them hither, Jarl Rannar's man Swinne. Fighting against Fate is meaningless.'

'You and your vague-speak.' The pockmarked man snorted and spat into the fire.

Muus avoided looking at the man. When the name Rannar fell, he had felt the Holderling beside him stiffen. Rannar of Westhal, whose lands lay far to the southeast, was a declared enemy of Jarl Dettrich and thus Kjelle's father. Rannar was an ambitious and unscrupulous man, with followers suited to his nature. *We'll have to be careful,* Muus thought, with a fleeting glance at the armed warriors. *One wrong word and our blood will flow. It's well they don't know who we are.*

While they passed between the men and the fire, one of the soldiers stuck his leg out. Muus stumbled and could just grab Kjelle's shoulder to prevent a fall. The ulvhednar gave Muus a blank stare and the tension mounted. But Muus said nothing. Amid the roaring laughter of the wolf warriors their escort led the two wanderers to the back.

In a separate room they found an elderly woman, reclining in an alcove. When the door closed behind them, their escort lowered her hood. To his surprise, Muus saw that the escort was a girl, not a man as he had thought. She bowed to the older woman. 'The searchers, Lady.' Then she retired into a back corner of the room.

'Welcome,' said the elderly woman. 'Pardon me for receiving you lying down; my legs cannot carry me. I am Asgisla, the Völva of Belisheim. Your coming was expected, Shardheld.'

'May the Gods be with you,' said Muus, greeting her upright as a free man. 'Harbard sent us here.'

The Völva smiled. 'He was correct, as always.' She gestured to a chest against the wall. 'Pull that closer and sit with me.' She waited until Muus and Kjelle had complied. 'I am sorry for not letting you rest after your journey. You have seen the warriors in the hall. They have waited almost half a day for a prophecy. I kept them waiting because I knew you would come, and I had to see you first. I know why you are here. Yet, I want to hear the story from your mouth, Shardheld.'

Muus nodded. He felt calm, safe in this dimly lit room. The gray eyes of the Völva were warm and understanding. He told the story as he had the old one-eye and, like Harbard, the Völva listened with such intensity that only the best of skalds aroused in their audience.

'You have the skyshard,' said she when Muus had finished. His hand went to the pouch around his neck, but the Völva shook her head.

'I do not need to see him, Shardheld. I know he is there. About him, we should talk. That does not bother him; nothing I can say will keep him from his purpose.'

'Can that stone hear us?' said Kjelle with fear in his voice. 'By Odin, I said you should throw it away, you fool.'

'The skyshard cannot be discarded, Holderling,' said Asgisla imperturbable. 'Nor can he be lost, stolen or harmed in any way. Once someone has found him, they will stay together until the skyshard has reached its fulfillment, or the bearer dies. Muus has no choice left. He is the Shardheld.' She glanced at the girl who had risen to pluck at the sputtering wick of an oil lamp until it burned brighter.

'Who or what is that Shardheld?' said Muus.

'That is a good question.' The Völva folded her hands on the blanket. 'When the new Gods had just ousted the old Powers, Chaos reigned in the lands. The Gods saw this with dismay, because Chaos threatened their plans for the world. They decided to create Order, so that the people would be united; far away, in the south of the world, stood a castle, the Wisborg. It rose up high on a peak above a deep gorge, in a region of wooded mountains and fast-flowing rivers. Here, twin boys were born, Karos and Kalman. Their people are unknown to us, but they descended from Godly stock, for the boys grew up to be strong and wise. When Karos became a man, he went into the world. He was a mighty warrior and succeeded in bringing the troubled lands under his dominion. Around the Wisborg, he founded the city of Rom, capital of the Eternal Empire. There he reigned long and just. At his side was Kalman, his brother and a great scholar, master of all magic. He wrote the Laws Karos implemented. After long years, Kalman died childless. His followers buried him in the depths of the caverns under the city of Rom. On his grave, they placed a monolith, the Kalmanir, which was infused with Kalman's magic wisdom. From that day, all the power of Wisewomen and -men in the lands of Rom sprang from that stone pillar.' Asgisla paused and looked at Muus, who stared back motionless. 'The glory of Rom has passed, but the power we use is still a gift from the Kalmanir. However, the strength of the monolith is not infinite. Whenever five times five times five generations have come and gone, the Kalmanir needs to be replenished. To that end, the Gods send a skyshard into the world, a piece of the blue sky. He or she who first puts a hand to this shard, is the Shardheld, whose fate it will be to unite the skyshard with the Kalmanir. That is no easy thing, the way and the task are dangerous for those of insufficient power. And thus we have a problem.'

Until now, Muus listened in silence, but at this, he had to swallow.

The lamplight reflected in Asgisla's eyes as she gave him a fixed stare. 'All earlier Shardhelds were mighty Wisewomen or great scholars: people with strength and experience. This is the first time the Shardheld is both a young man and a thrall.'

'What!' Muus colored. 'I'm no thrall.'

The Völva raised her hand. 'The threads of your lives I can read while they are spun,' said she. 'Kjelle Almansen, your past, present and future are not secret to me.'

The Holderling paled. Sweat beaded on his forehead and his mouth hung open.

Asgisla ignored his fear. 'Of Muus I see ...' Now her voice faltered a moment. 'Only the present. There is a haze over what has been and what will be is a fiery cave that obscures images.'

The Völva beckoned the girl. 'This is Birthe,' said Asgisla. 'She is my arms, legs, eyes and ears outside this room. Birthe, bring me two thimbles.'

Moments later the girl came back with two thumb-sized bronze cups. One she offered the Völva and the other to Muus. 'Here,' said she in a voice bordering on hostility.

Muus looked from the cup to her face. 'What's in it?'

'Just drink it, boy,' Birthe snapped.

Asgisla smiled. 'Be calm, girl. Do not fear, Muus. This water joins you and me in a dream that I can read. It will tell me if your powers are sufficient to bear your load. Drink, Shardheld.' With a practiced motion, she poured the contents of her thumb in the back of her throat.

Muus brought his cup to the mouth. It smelled strange, of unknown herbs. With his eyes closed, he drank the water. The taste was bittersweet...

He is drifting through the sky. Around him, clouds spun from endless threads, disappearing in the distance. Then, his vision changes.

Faceless men and women wander through the mist. Some have mouths that open and close silently, others only an eye or an ear. All are unrecognizable. The wooden prow of a longship slides into view. Fierce men with axes throw themselves onto the faceless ones. Their mouths open wider and there is blood, fire. A leather arm drags a little boy away from the faceless ones. The closed mouth of the boy screams through his eyes.

The longship dances on the green seas. Waves, high and foaming, chase the ship continuously, while the rowers, their oars resting, cling to their banks. The sail is tight and round, so it seems that the painted bear stands ready to attack. A little boy, shivering from cold, stands tied to the mast. There are more captured children on board, but he is the only one who doesn't cry. The bear on the sail is Skid Largassen's sign, the Viking of Helmshaven.

Wooden houses, mud houses, thatched roofs. There are wind and rain, the lapping sea against the piers. The streets are made of wooden planks on the tidewater, and sheep roam on the high ground. Helmshaven, near Harkoy.

There is a smoky hall, dark and smelling of stale beer. Smoking torches illuminate wailing children. The little boy still won't cry; his mouth is closed. Only his eyes are screaming. Men shout unintelligible words. Jingling coins go from hand to hand and one by one, the crying children disappear. A younger Hagen, dressed in a new coat of white wolf's fur, takes the little boy outside. The slave market of Helmshaven.

In darkness he drifts, alone.

Kjelle watched how Muus' eyes rolled away, and the small hairs on his arms stood up. Hagen's eyes did just so when he died. *No!* The cold sweat broke him out at the thought. He needed Muus. He stared at the unconscious slave, his mind in confusion and his heart beating so fast that he thought he was choking. From the first moment, when his father had given Muus to him as a present, he'd loathed the boy. That black hair masking a pale face, the straight shoulders so unafraid. He looked like a svartalf and he never cried, not even when Kjelle slapped him. He was so small and thin, such an arrogant mouse. Never-Frightened Muus. Look at how he had killed that snow wolf. He had never before held a sword in his hands, but the animal died, not Muus. Muus was strong for two. Muus had to live.

The old Völva moved her hands and she sang so softly that he could not hear the words. Muus moved back and forth with the music, his face blank as one of the stone statues in Siga's room. Kjelle's stomach shrank at the sight. This was unnatural. Muus' magic, his helpless state, was unmanly. No Nord should bring himself in such a position. Muus was no Nord, but still ... magic is for women.

'The Völva has spoken,' said Birthe. Unnoticed, she had approached and looked down at Muus. 'Pick him up; I'll bring you two to another room. A few hours' sleep and he'll be all right. Then the Völva will tell you her findings.'

Through a hidden back door, she took them through the cold to a small hut near the exit. 'You'll find some straw pallets. I'll bring food and drink,' said the girl. 'Try to rest. When the time is there, I'll come for you. Stay inside until then. Avoid the wolf warriors of Westhal.'

Kjelle winced. 'Rannar's men are no friends of my house,'

The girl looked at him. 'Of none,' said she, before she closed the door behind her.

Kjelle laid Muus roughly on one of the pallets. With his fists clenched, he looked at the sword on his belt. Hagen's sword, so large for such a little man. Would he...? No. Kjelle shivered. The sword had brought Muus luck, better let him keep it, you never knew. He stretched out on a second pallet and slept.

Rough hands shook Kjelle until he opened his eyes. 'Wake up.' A voice whispered. 'Freya, help me; do wake up.' It was Birthe, her face wet with tears and with blood from a long gash on her right eyebrow.

'You're hurt.'

'That's for later. We must flee. Quick, get ready.'

Kjelle felt his heart pounding in his chest. 'What's happening?' he said, while he fastened his snowshoes and grabbed in the dark for his backpack.

'Swinne!' The girl's face was a snarling mask of hate. 'That mangy rat killed Asgisla. His men are plundering the house; we must go before they come here.'

Kjelle began to sweat, 'Muus! Lazy bastard.' He shook the limp body. 'He won't wake up.'

'Control yourself.' Birthe's voice was like a whiplash. 'It's the dream water. You must carry him.'

Kjelle made a face. 'Carry him?'

'You don't like him. That doesn't matter, pick him up.'

The Holderling bent down and lifted the unconscious Muus from the ground. 'He does not weigh much.'

'Easy! You don't have to break his arm.' Birthe looked out the door. 'There's no one. Come, quickly. '

Like two frightened shadows, they fled into the dark. It was snowing as they hurried through the forest, Kjelle with Muus over his shoulders and Birthe, deep in her cloak, silent. The ruddy glow of Belisheim's torches faded in the twilight and soon there was nothing but snow and the creaking of overloaded branches. Kjelle lost all sense of time and direction. Blindly, he followed Birthe until they came to the gaping mouth of a cave. A familiar smell greeted him, bringing memories he hastily repressed. Beside him, Birthe raised her hands and began to chant. She waited and listened, but nothing moved. 'It's empty.'

Kjelle followed her inside and looked around. The cave was wide enough for them to sleep in and so deep that it protected them from the wind. He stooped and laid Muus down. 'Do you know where we are?'

The girl looked at him. Her bloodied face was gray, her eyes red from crying and her hands gripped the staff she carried as if it rooted her to the firm earth. 'I know the whole area. A bear lived here, but hunters slew it last summer. I expected the cave to be empty; its spirit is still strong in here.'

'Will they find us?' Kjelle felt his voice trembling. Birthe brushed her sleeve across her nose; tears glistened in her eyelashes. 'I don't think so. They were mad with mead and beer. Besides, it's snowing hard; our footprints will be long gone. No, even their wolf-noses won't find us.'

The Holderling relaxed slightly. 'Then we're safe for a while. Where did you get that wound?'

'One of Swinne's men wanted to rape me. I objected, but I was a bit slow. The Fates were with me, though, his knife was meant for my throat.' Her face tried to smile. 'He was so eager; he grabbed me with his pants down. When I left him, he was trying to get his entrails back inside.' She brought her fingers to the wound, but then hesitated. 'How big is the cut?'

'From your eye to above the nose,' said Kjelle. 'It's still bleeding.'

Birthe took from her coat a tightly wound roll of cloth and a small bag of dried leaves. 'Can you bind it?'

Kjelle nodded. 'My father wanted me to know something of battlefield healing.'

'A sensible thought. Wrap some yarrow leaves over the cut, they'll help it heal.'

Kjelle swallowed. Wisewoman Siga had shown him how, but never with a real wound. While he bound the long bandage over the cut, he looked at the girl. She saw him not, with empty eyes she stared at the snow outside. She'd been confident, so frighteningly self-assured. With the pack on her back, the quiver on her hip, a sheathed bow over the shoulder and on her belt a hunting knife as long as his forearm, she looked more like a warrior than a Völva. Disemboweling her rapist... he shivered. 'What have you got under your cloak?' he asked, laying the last knot in the bandage. 'It's moving.'

Birthe gasped and grabbed the bag. 'Oh, little man,' said she, 'you must keep your arms inside. It's too cold to wave.'

'A babe?' Kjelle's voice was shrill. 'You're carrying a babe with you?'

CHAPTER 5 - AMBUSH

The bridal party was just two days underway from Jonthal on the coast to Leidwald, deep in the forests of Dalland. Two oxen pulled the wagon over the frozen road. One side of the leather hood was open, so that Swanfrid could converse with her new husband.

Young Ajkell Gudrofsen followed with the rear guard, his eyes alert and his hand never far away from his sword. Not that he expected any trouble. The sons of Gudrof came from a famous clan of bear totem warriors, and they were battle-ready even in their sleep. That was why Leidwald had hired their youngest son as bodyguard to their Holderling.

Ajkell looked at his master and mistress. He grinned. The bride, an avid huntress, was sulking at being cooped up in the with her young thrall maid and her wedding gifts, and Meili, her husband, was doing his best to coax her out of it. The Holderling was in a good mood and no wonder; he was young, healthy and proud of his new wife. The wedding had been a great success. Only the absence of Holder Brandr, Meili's father, had marred it, but the old man's heart wasn't strong enough for a long trip. Now there was a second feast awaiting them when they got home.

Ajkell's gaze went to the headman, a giant warrior in a mail shirt, with copper rings in his braided hair and his three-forked beard. His face looked carved in stone, his mouth grim.

It started to snow. Ajkell looked at the sky and sneezed. Rattling, the wagon went onward. The wheels crunched through the snow and the oxen trudged unperturbed. Holderling Meili said something to his young wife. It must have been funny, because Ajkell heard her laugh.

The young bear warrior looked up. Something felt wrong. The headman had noticed it, too. He looked around, his hands clasping the grip of his mighty ax. Then the snowflakes became spikes and the large man died, his body pierced by a dozen arrows.

Before the headman fell, Ajkell sprang forward and dragged the Holderling from his horse. 'Get under the wagon. Leave the fighting to me.' But a shaft had burrowed into Meili's back and the blood from his mouth ran down Ajkell's bear coat.

Around him, only three soldiers were still fighting, The young bride jumped from the back of the wagon with the new short bow that was her father's gift. She shot at the grim shadows in the snow and killed two of them, when others rounded the wagon and fell on her from behind. Ajkell ran to her aid and swung his sword. The first attacker collapsed with a bemused expression on his rolling head. While the young bear warrior turned to the next, he saw how one of the attackers stuck his short sword into Swanfrid's back. Her last arrow disappeared aimlessly amongst the snowflakes. Blood welled under her breasts, her festive robe colored pink and Ajkell yelled in desperation. His opponent went down with his helmet and his skull split. Panting, Ajkell looked around for the killer of his mistress. Then the stars in the sky burst in his head and all went black.

What made him wake up, were two hands plucking at his belt. He groaned and hit out with one arm, as if he wanted to chase away troublesome flies. Above him, he heard a muffled cry, and he opened his eyes. A child, a boy with a dirty face and fierce eyes stared at him. He had blood on his hands, his cheeks and his mismatched clothes. On his greasy hair sat Swanfrid's bridal wreath and in his fist, he had a knife.

'No,' said Ajkell and his hand grabbed the wrist with the knife. 'No, son of a lice-eaten bitch, keep your paws off me.'

A big grin spread over the filthy young face. 'You're alive. *He* thought you were dead and his men left. Yet you're alive. Let me go, oh Thor with the mighty muscles. Enjoy your life and let me go, before I lose him.'

Ajkell gritted his teeth against the pain in his head. 'Who's him?' he asked. 'And who are you?'

'I am nothing, Thor. I am a shadow. Too insignificant to kill. Or maybe I'm already dead.'

'You're not dead,' said Ajkell. 'I feel your arm, your heart beats. Do you have a name?'

The boy laughed again, his head cocked. 'Call me Hraab.'

'Raven,' said Ajkell grim faced. 'Robber of the dead. A good name, child. Who is your 'he'?'

'He's Vulf. Mrrrarh,' said the boy with a nice imitation of a snarling wolf. 'That's what he called himself.'

'Raven and Wolf. Tell me more about Vulf. '

The boy's face twisted. 'He is Death with the face of a young man, my brother's age. The Wolf serves a great lord in the south, a Jarl.' He leaned over and whispered, 'Rannar the Snake.'

Ajkell sat upright and the boy squeaked when his hand was squeezed. 'Rannar?' said the young warrior. 'How do you know?'

'While I was dead on the floor, I heard them talking. Boasting about the rewards Rannar would give them for their deeds.'

'Rannar. He's a friend of my master's father-in-law. Why would he do this?'

'The snake bites his friends as well,' said Hraab. 'He's made that way.'

Ajkell pulled the boy toward him. 'You speak the truth? I'll kill you if you're lying, child. '

'I am already dead, Thor. I died when Vulf destroyed my family. I lay beneath my brother's body, next to my father and my mother. Then, as with you, the Norns spun me a bit of life and I awoke. The house burned, but I managed to get away. Vulf's troop was not far and I followed.'

'Why?'

The boy shrugged. 'I am like a draug, a walking dead. Following them gives me a purpose. I eat what they leave behind, sleep in the snow and wait for an opportunity.' A grin broke across his face. 'They know I'm there. Vulf thinks it is funny. He waves at me when he sees me and at times, his men leave some food behind. As if they want me to follow.' He sighed. 'When I find him alone he'll have my little hawk in his back.'

'Another beast?'

'Let me go and I will show you.'

'I'll let you go if you won't run away.'

The boy laughed. 'I will not run. Our goals are the same, Thor. '

Ajkell released him and the boy shook his fingers a few times.

'Good. The hawk flies.' He moved his hand and a moment later a small throwing ax sat trembling in a tree about ten yards away. 'He found his prey.'

The young warrior nodded. 'A useful animal, child.' He stood and stared at the corpses. 'The heirs of two Holds lie here dead. Two rich lands with old rulers robbed of their successor.' His voice was cold, stripped of all laughter. 'You see the noble lord? That was Meili Brandrsen, Holderling of Leidwald, whose life was mine to protect. The lady whose garland you wear was Swanfrid, Jonthal's heiress and Meili's bride of three days. See their paleness, their blood. I have failed, raven's child, failed in my oath. I should have fallen before them, but I'm still alive. With them died my honor, the honor of clan Gudrofsen.'

'You're like me, brother draug,' said the boy. 'Vulf's death restores your honor, and - perhaps - my life.'

Ajkell searched for his sword and found it lying in the snow, with a foot and a half of the point broken off. 'How in Hel's name...' Then he saw the point, wedged between two rocks. 'I must have fallen upon it.' His sword was broken like his honor. Without thought, he lifted it to the sky. 'This blade will not be repaired while my revenge is undone.' He returned the broken sword to its scabbard and turned around. 'Help me lay out my lord and lady. I can't leave them like this. Then we'll follow the Wolf. '

'Good,' said the boy. 'Thor and the raven together.'

Belisheim couldn't be far. "Just follow the river," the villagers had said, "you can't miss it. The Völva is a great lady, she'll feed you well and you'll sleep dry for a night." Tuuri grinned. Hot food was promising, but more important was the question his master wanted him to ask her. He was to offer money for the answer. One hundred gold coins, carefully put away under the false bottom of his saddlebag. Another was to ask the same question, but his argument was force of arms. Tuuri grinned; he thought his own way much more pleasant.

For the second time the smell of burning filled his nostrils. He slowed his horse to a walk, ready to flee at the slightest hint of danger. He saw the glowing remains of burned-out buildings through the trees. Someone had dared to touch the greatest Völva in the world? Tuuri followed the Gods of his mother and to him the Wisewomen were extensions of Freya herself, inviolate.

He stared at the ruins of the Völva's place. It refused to penetrate his brain. They killed the Wisewoman? His eyes went to the men among the trees. Most of them were sleeping, drunk on plunder and mayhem. One man, older, bearded, with the same markings as Vulf wore, regarded him bleary-eyed. 'Whor you?' said he. 'Ya look a Fynnikin, pup.'

'I am. And who are you? Did you do this fool deed?'

The man bristled. 'Fool? We burned the witch, the lying arrogant whore. Whaddayar doin' here?'

'I'm Jarl Rannar's messenger. I was to ask the Völva a question, in case the first asker with the soldiers failed. Were you that one?'

The man spat a glob of saliva in Tuuri's direction. 'I didna fail, Fynnikin pup. I'm Swinne, Tarkynn of the Azdainii. I can't fail. She kept me waitin' for nearly a day and then... then she said no. So we killed her.' He slumped back against the tree he was sitting under, and belched.

Tuuri shivered. He felt his world collapsing around him. First Vulf and now Swinne. His past, his pride, it was all a lie. He straightened. 'This was not what the Jarl intended. He wanted her advice.'

'Then the more fool he,' said the drunken Tarkynn, scratching under his wolfs cap. 'You don' trust a lyin' woman, pup.'

'I'll have to report this.' Tuuri could barely contain his anger.

Swinne stared at him, his eyes red as the embers of the smoldering house. His grin was unpleasant, showing rows of rotting teeth. 'You do that, little lickspittle. That damned Jarl of yours pays me, he don' tells me what to do. I'm a Fynni chief. Naagh, get away from 'ere while you're still whole, you bloddy half-breed. Your prattle starts to irritate me.'

Without a word, Tuuri wheeled his horse around and rode back into the snowy woods. Panic gnawed at his heart. *I must go home. The Jarl needs to know what's happening here. His whole plan is becoming undone by those animals. Half-breed.* The word he hated most and the one that was the truest.

CHAPTER 6 - MORE PERILS

Muus returned to the world on gusts of consciousness. Slowly he felt the hard floor against his back. 'Kjelle?'

'You're awake.'

Blinking his eyes, Muus recognized the face of the Holderling.

With Kjelle's strong arm in his back, Muus sat up. 'A cave?' Then he saw Birthe. 'You here? What happened?'

'Swinne,' said the two together. Birthe's reaction was the fiercest and Muus looked at the girl's bandaged face.

'You're the Völva's disciple. Did you leave the lady alone?'

'She's dead.' A lament sung from Birthe's lips. With her arms around the bag on her lap she rocked back and forth, her eyes turned inward.

'Swinne's men have killed Asgisla and her people,' said Kjelle. 'While they plundered Belisheim, Birthe came to warn me that we had to flee. I couldn't wake you.'

'And then?' Muus clenched his fists.

'Then I carried you. That meager body of yours doesn't weigh much.' Kjelle looked at him obliquely. 'You're eating too little.'

'A hunk of bread, now and then,' said Muus. Then he grasped Kjelle's hand. 'Thank you.'

The Holderling snorted. 'I didn't want to lose you, Bryt. You're the only one who can confirm whom I am.'

Muus patted Kjelle's arm. 'I'll swear a thousand oaths, Holderling.' A feeling of depression came over him and he looked at the snow outside the cave. 'Now I'll never know what the Völva learned about me.'

'Of course you will.' Birthe sat upright, her face expressionless. 'I am a Völva, after all.'

Muus looked at her. 'Don't you have to be old for that?'

'I've been married,' snapped the girl. 'Old enough, if you're born with the power.'

'Muus,' said Kjelle and he sounded strained. 'She has a babe with her.'

Birthe lifted the bundle of furs from her bosom and through its folds a tiny, serious face with blue eyes looked at Muus. 'He's called Búi,' said she. 'Búi Birthesen. My son, my name. His father almost killed the bear that lived in this cave, but the bear won. Barn was no hunter. He hoped to impress me; instead, he made me a widow. The fool.' She wiped her tears away. 'I was three months pregnant, when I went and killed his bear for him, just as long as we'd been married.' She cradled the little one in her arms. 'I could find another man, but I don't want to. Never again.' From her belt the girl took a slender metal rod, about as long as her forearm. 'I'm of the völur now, wand-wed. I don't need a husband.' Búi began to cry. She unbuttoned her coat and her vest. Moments later, the newborn's mouth had found her nipple and sucked his meal down. 'He's always hungry,' said she. 'Just like his father.'

Muus looked at her. 'I'm sorry.'

'So am I.' The girl sounded bitter. 'We were too young.' Almost angrily she gripped her wand. 'We were talking about you and what the Völva knew of you.'

'All right,' said Muus. 'Tell me what the lady discovered.'

Birthe looked at him. 'You're a Bryt.'

'I know,' said Muus. 'I've heard her say so.'

'You were stolen by Skid Largassen, the one named Bearjaw, the Viking of Helmshaven.'

'I saw him in my dream,' said Muus. 'Images of the raid, his longship with the bear on its sail, of Helmshaven and the slave market.'

'You have the power of magic.'

'Yes.'

'But not enough.'

Muus jolted upright. 'What does that mean? '

'That the skyshard will take over your mind. Unless...'

'Unless what?' said Kjelle.

'Unless your mind is freed from the spell that has been cast upon you.'

'What spell?'

'I don't know.' Birthe held out her arm. 'Give me your hand.'

Her grip was harder than he expected, almost masculine. The contact caused a tingling that went through his shoulder. He resisted the urge to scratch and waited.

Birthe nodded. 'There is a threshold where I cannot cross. Someone has put a spell on your past. Your memories are still there, but unreadable. The power of this spell is different from ours. My lady couldn't have helped you, so I am not even going to try. I think you can find help only in your own lands.'

Muus jerked his hand away. 'No!' For the first time he felt panic rising.

'You've no choice, Shardheld. You must go to Brytanna. '

'But he can't,' stammered Kjelle. 'Muus must help me. He is my ...' The right word would not come.

Birthe gave a thin smile. 'He is no thrall, Holderling. The Shardheld must go through the world freely.'

Kjelle made an impatient gesture. 'He's from my household. If he says he's a free man, I won't contradict him. He deserves that much.'

'When he returns to Brytanna, he is legally free.'

'But he must help me,' cried Kjelle.

'We'll go to Eidungruve first.' Muus hesitated. 'I too want to know if it still exists.'

'You can't stay there,' said Birthe.

'I know that.' Muus looked at Kjelle. 'Even if your land and your father turn out to have been spared, I must go on. If necessary as a runaway.'

Kjelle's eyes burned. Then he nodded. 'Does anyone know where to find that standing stone Muus must seek? Somewhere in the south, the Völva said.' His voice was casual, but his eyes betrayed his strain.

Birthe stared at her wand. 'I know what the legends say. The Kalmanir stands in the Cave of the Flaming Well under the ruins of Rom, in the Gorge of the Two Kings far in the Desert of Orange and Red, in Falrom, in the south of the world.'

'Falrom,' whispered the Holderling, deadly pale.

Muus sat rigid as a sun-touched troll and stared at the sudden vision of a glowing landscape of smoke and fire. 'I see it,' said he. 'With the skyshard in my hand I see it. Orange and red are the rocks. Fiery earthblood flows through the riverbeds and the mountains are vomiting flames. It is hot.' He let go of the skyshard and sighed. 'I must go there, Kjelle. The skyshard tells me. He knows the way.'

The young Holderling stared at Muus with a look of awe, and almost of submission.

Then Muus jumped up. 'But first we go to Eidungruve.'

Birthe tucked little Búi back in the furs on her back. 'I'm coming with you.'

Muus saw the shock on Kjelle's face. 'With that child? We sleep in the snow, we have to catch our food and we could be dead before Sun's chariot returns in the sky,' said the Holderling.

'My father was a hunter,' said Birthe with pride. 'Since my fifth winter I lived with him in the woods, so the snow is nothing new for me.' Her hand went to the bow in its sheath on her hip. 'This was my father's. A snow bear caught him from up close, while he was crapping. We'd had no idea that the beast was near. The bow hung from a branch. I grabbed it and ran.'

'Your father was already dead?' said Kjelle.

Birthe's eyes glittered. 'You think me a coward?' she snapped. 'Yes, he was quite dead when I left.' She clenched her fists. 'My arms lacked the power to avenge him, so I fled into the forest. Fate had a moment of weakness that time and led my feet to Belisheim, where the Völva took me in as her apprentice. I was ten years old. Asgisla saw my power and taught me of her wisdom. A little, enough to set me on the path of Song and Chant. Then Barn came, in search of glory. He had just such blue eyes as Búi. My lady comforted me as a mother when he died. And now ...'

'Now what?'

'Now the Völva is gone.' She turned wildly, scattering snow from her cloak. 'Both my men I lost to a bear, my lady to a beast crueler than that. All I have left is Búi. He lives and dies with me.' She took a deep breath and calmed. 'We shan't be a burden to you, Shardheld.'

Birthe was as good as her word. She led them unerringly through dark woods and snowstorms, until they reached a road.

Kjelle peered through the slatted wooden snow goggles they'd made. 'This must be King Hurald's Way.'

Birthe nodded. 'The Royal road to the south. Be glad it's winter. In summer it's a muddy midge-fest.'

'Well done,' said Muus, but Birthe stared at a bend in the road and didn't answer. Instead, she pointed. 'Something's amiss over there.' Through the edge of the forest she led them further, until they came to a large wagon blocking the road, with dead oxen, and the bodies of guards partly covered by snow.

'There was an ambush.' Kjelle sounded shaken.

'A bridal party.' Birthe voice was hoarse, while her hand went as of itself to the babe on her back. 'Look.'

Under the wagon lay side by side a young couple, pale and frozen. He in a long, dark red tunic of fine cloth, she in what must have been a wedding gown, with ribbons and sewed-on flowers, blood-drenched from a gaping wound under her breasts. 'There must have been a survivor. A servant, someone who has taken the trouble to lay out the master and mistress.' Muus looked around, at the wagon, the fallen soldiers and back to the dead pair, trying to see how it had happened. 'This wasn't robbery. Look at those warriors. All their weapons and equipment are still scattered around. What bandit would leave that big guy's battle ax behind? It must be worth a small fortune.'

'But who'd do such a thing?'

Birthe swore so bitterly that Kjelle looked at her. 'Green-and-yellow arrow feathers.'

'Those are Herigel's colors.' Kjelle's face turned red. 'Herigel kills in Dalland? Jarl Dettrich should know about this.'

'Swinne's bowmen had the same color in their quivers,' said Birthe.

A deathly silence fell.

'I don't understand,' said Kjelle. 'Swinne is Rannar's man. Why would he ambush someone in our jarldom, under Herigel's colors? In Thor's name, why? '

Muus threw him an swift glance. 'To make Jarl Dettrich think Herigel attacks him?'

Kjelle's mouth fell open. 'But that would mean war.'

'Rannar has his eyes on the throne,' said Birthe.

'How do you know?'

'That's what Swinne came to Belisheim for. He wanted a prediction from the Völva about his master's chances, should the King die. My lady refused. That was why Swinne killed her.'

Kjelle nodded. 'So that's it. Waldrich of Herigel is one of the King's staunchest supporters. With him out of the way, the King would be alone.'

'My, you have paid attention between bedding the girls,' said Muus.

Kjelle spat into the snow. 'I am the Holderling, Bryt. Most folks didn't know it, but my father's health was failing. That groin injury was worse than he'd admit; it was killing him. Of course I had my ears open.' He looked around. 'That giant one was no ordinary warrior, his equipment is too expensive. He must have been the headman.'

'Even so, he died without fighting,' said Muus. 'The arrows totally surprised him.'

Kjelle went over to where the big warrior lay. 'Twelve shafts. That must have meant instant death.' He snatched a large, beautifully engraved ax from the snow. 'I want this one.'

Muus looked at him. 'You can't have it. That ax is a masterpiece and far too recognizable. You don't want someone taking you for one of those murderers.'

Kjelle sighed. 'You're right. But I must have weapons.'

'Take them off the soldiers. Half of all Norden uses the same.'

Kjelle muttered something, but grabbed two axes from the frozen ground and stuck them on his belt.

Birthe made a stifled sound. When the other two joined her, they found her staring down at a young girl, thrown spread-legged into the back of the wagon.'

'She must have been a thrall,' said Kjelle awkwardly.

Birthe turned to him and her eyes glittered. 'She was nothing but a child. Not a...a *thing,* to be used and discarded.'

'You're right.' Muus' voice sounded bitter. 'Even a thrall shouldn't be raped.'

Kjelle looked confused. 'I didn't mean that.'

'She's frozen.' Birthe tried to move the dead girl, but she stuck to the bottom of the wagon.'

'Better leave her,' said Muus. 'When we get to Jarl Dettrich, we'll tell him about this and he'll surely make arrangements.'

Birthe stifled a sob and nodded. She sang a few words, almost inaudible and made the sign of Freya over the dead body. 'May Helheim be kinder to you than the world was, girl.'

'We need food,' said Kjelle, still red-faced. 'Would there be anything left in the wagon?'

Birthe glared at him, but she said nothing.

'I'll have a look.' Muus scrambled into the wagon and started going through the bags and chests. 'There's plenty food. And look, here's a tent. The Holderling and his lady didn't sleep in the wagon then.' Quickly he passed bread, frozen meat, cheese, dried apples and a little bag full of mixed nuts to Kjelle. Finally he dropped the rolled-up tent over the side. 'We need bindings to carry it.'

Without a word, Kjelle cut some lengths of leather out of the ox's harness and fastened the tent to Muus' shoulders. Then he shrugged into the straps of his own, now well-filled backpack.

'We'll go cross-country,' said Birthe. 'That's less conspicuous.'

'You think whoever murdered them is still around?'

The girl glanced at Kjelle. 'No, but I want to be sure.'

Kjelle nodded and slowly they made their way, weighed down by their load.

Tuuri's happy expectations had vanished. The longed for meetings with his kin had turned into a disaster. His fingers touched the symbol on his cheek. His mark of shame. *Fynni. They're nothing but animals and murderers.* Suddenly he shot upright in the saddle. *My father. Was he, too, one of those?* The idea made him want to puke. He had never felt so dirty in his life. Was that why mother never spoke of his father? The thought brought tears to his eyes. He had to go home, to confront her with it. And the Jarl, who entrusted his great plan to these beasts, was he to be betrayed?'

He followed King Hurald's Way. He felt a need to gallop back to Helmshaven and sail home. But the road was bad here, and anything faster than a stroll was asking for broken legs.

The horse halted and shook her head.

'What is it, girl?' said Tuuri, patting the animal's neck. Then he saw through the bend in the road a large wagon athwart the road. His horse didn't budge, so he dismounted and led the animal forward. He noted the little snowy mounds and the two bodies under the wagon. The fresh tracks leading to and from the wagon made his heart beat faster.. He froze and listened, but the only sounds were the creaking of branches and the rustle of snow coming down from a tree. Slightly reassured he walked towards the wagon. A young girl sprawled in the back, her dress turned up and bare legs twisted in a last struggle. He touched her and was shocked by the frozen hardness of her body. *Poor, pretty child. You shouldn't have had to die like this.* His eyes found a green-and-yellow arrow standing in the side of the wagon. Vulf's colors. He saw more arrows and all at once, he understood. It was a trick, using false colors to sow discord between the local Jarl and a neighbor. Only they had chosen the wrong victims. Killing a lordling and his retinue was an invitation for civil war. That wouldn't help Rannar. He cursed Vulf and his brainless followers.

With soft words he led his horse past the snow-covered bodies and continued his way.

A few hours later he came to a sharp bend in the road, with a side-path leading into the mountains. A standing stone pointed to a settlement he'd never heard of, Eidungruve. Tuuri halted. He desperately wanted to see people. Ordinary, living, decent people, to talk with and perhaps to laugh a bit.

After an hour or so, he saw the contours of a palisade in the distance. His horse stopped abruptly. 'What is it?' Then he saw the snow-covered heap in the middle of the path, with a green-and-yellow arrow sticking out of it. He looked around, but there was nobody in sight.

Tuuri slid from the saddle and led his unwilling horse into the woods. Out of sight from the road, he bound the animal to a tree. A few steps away he called. *Sha'akaii.*

His massive totem bear appeared with as little enthusiasm as before to be called from its warm world. The animal stared at him. Tuuri spread his hands. *There's trouble brewing, my friend. Lend me your form, oh mighty Sha'akaii. I have need of stealth.*

The bear moved up to him, topping him by a good head. Tuuri gripped its rough fur and felt himself change. For a moment he was dizzy. Then, in the shape of an invisible bear, he hurried away to the Hold.

Oh Gods. The sight of the rows of hacked-off heads made his stomach turn. He stared up at the unfamiliar yellow-and-green banner on the walls. *Vulf again! If it gets out that Rannar's men are behind this carnage, the whole country will turn against him.* Tuuri shuddered, feeling vulnerable. Unseen; he slipped through the open gate. Inside the palisade, the snow was blood-soaked. The first barracks he opened contained heaps of dead men, headless and discarded. The other buildings showed signs of plundering and wanton rampage. He had saved the main hall for last. Here would be Vulf with his men.

Carefully, he peered inside. He counted over seventy warriors, drinking, sleeping, and fornicating with abandon on exhausted female prisoners. *Beasts*, he thought. He saw Vulf, lounging in a box chair, legs stretched out in front of him, staring at him with a sarcastic grin on his face. *He sees me!* Tuuri fled from the longhouse, back into the relative safety of the forest. He changed back into his own form and waves of sickness overcame him. He spewed in the snow until his stomach was empty. *How could he see me?* The thought ran through his head, chasing its own tail. What was Vulf? Fighting panic, Tuuri jumped in the saddle and fled. *To Helmshaven. Jarl Rannar must be warned.*

CHAPTER 7 - HOMECOMING

The next afternoon, ten days and nights since they had climbed the Silfjall, Kjelle and Muus came home. In the distance loomed the palisade of Eidungruve and the Holderling heaved a deep sigh. But before he could say something, Birthe raised her hand. 'Wait.'

A little further on an arrow stuck in the snow. A long, iron arrow with green-and-yellow feathers.

Carefully they went forward. Near the arrow, Muus' foot hit something that didn't budge and he knelt down. With his hands, he cleared away the snow.

'A karl.' Kjelle's voice sounded strained. 'Damn, it's one of ours.'

'Shot in the back,' said Birthe.

The others stared at her.

'Swinne? Could he have arrived here so fast?' Kjelle's hands went to his axes.

Birthe shook her head. 'When we fled Belisheim, Swinne's men were still looting. Blood-mad and drunk they were, they'd be going nowhere that night, nor the next day. They can't ever have overtaken us.'

Kjelle mustered the walls with his gaze. 'No watchman in sight. The banner ... ' His eyes narrowed to slits. 'Those are Herigel's colors again. Come.'

They went through the forest, keeping out of sight of any watchers on the palisades.

'The avalanche hasn't reached the Hold. Of that at least your hands are clean,' said Muus in a whisper.

Kjelle glanced at him, but there was no relief on his face.

When they reached the front gate, he froze. 'No. Oh Thor, no.'

Beside him, Muus retched and struggled to keep his stomach down. On either side of the road from the gate was a row of stakes with heads. Heads of people he had known.

'My father?' Kjelle's breath labored as if he'd run a long distance. 'I don't see him, is my father there?'

Muus gritted his teeth and glanced along the horrible heads. Most were karls and freedmen, no women were among them. Then he saw the stake above the entrance, with the severed head of Holder Alman. He pointed and Kjelle's gaze followed his finger. The eyes of the Holderling opened wide and his lips began to scream. Muus slapped him hard in the face, twice. 'Quiet.'

Kjelle's mouth snapped shut.

'We must get away from here,' said Birthe. 'Come.'

With his hand on Kjelle's shoulder, Muus hurried him along the edge of the forest until they were out of sight of the Hold. The Holderling walked as a draug. His face was blank; his shoulder under Muus' hand felt rigid as a wooden plank and his feet stumbled over the snow-covered road.

Nearby, someone laughed. Another man answered and quickly Muus pulled Kjelle behind a clump of pine trees. Birthe slipped next to them and held up four fingers.

Four warriors came down the path, pulling a sled with the carcass of a deer. They joked like content men do, one of them boasting in a loud voice about the blonde girl he had taken and how she'd screamed and begged.

Kjelle moved from under Muus' arm, He dropped his backpack and gripped his axes. Before the other two could stop him, he yelled 'For Ema!' and threw himself on the warriors.

'O Thor,' snarled Muus, while he drew his sword.

The attack took the four ulvhednar completely by surprise. Kjelle made use of their momentary shock by laying the face of the boasting one open. Blood and brains splattered around while the man went down without a sound. Muus ran with his sword leveled in front of him like a spear. His target started to swing his ax and in a reflex, Muus ducked. He had forgotten the rolled-up tent on his back and the weight brought him off balance. His knee crashed into the side of the sled and with a cry, he pitched forward. In desperation, he swung his sword and his momentum pushed the blade deep into the guts of his opponent. The man screamed; a piercing sound that made Muus' blood run cold. Muus scrambled to his feet and struck blindly at the neck of the ulvhednar. The shrieking broke off. Panting, Muus looked around, with the sweat dripping from his face. He saw how Kjelle sprang at the third man, bellowing his anger, without regard for his own safety. The bandit tried to fend off the pounding blows, but he stood no chance. Kjelle turned his weapon and broke the man's jaw with the handle, after which he placed the ax in his enemy's forehead. The fourth man fled.

'Stop him,' said Muus to Birthe. 'Quickly, before he can sound the alarm.'

From Birthe's bow came a humming sound. For a second, the world seemed to hold its breath. Then the running man pitched forward. The virginal white around him turned red, and his legs jerked a last time.

'Nice shot,' said Muus.' Then he saw the tears running down her face. 'First kill?'

Birthe nodded as she returned her bow to her shoulder. Even so, she walked to her victim and broke off the plume of the arrow shaft. Then she went through his pockets.

Meanwhile Muus had put his arms around Kjelle. 'You have fought well,' said he. 'Your father would have been proud of you.'

Kjelle looked at him. His eyes were empty. Blood stuck to the front of his leather coat and speckled his face. 'Ema,' said he in a dead voice. He shuddered. Then he raised his ax. 'Flee, Rannar' he shouted. 'Run while you still can, because I come for you. I, Kjelle Almansen, promise you will pay.' Then he sank down on the edge of the sled and cried.

Muus let him be and followed Birthe's example.

'Who's Ema?' asked the girl

'The daughter of one of our karls. Kjelle was a bit sweet on her, as far as that goes by him.'

Birthe gave him a steely glance, but she didn't say anything.

The dead possessed little of value. A handful of coppers and some silver coins, a hunting knife and a dried rabbit's foot were all.

'Let's get away from here,' said Muus. 'By the time those four will be missed, we must be somewhere else.'

'We're going to Harkoy.' Kjelle jumped up, his face deathly pale. In his voice lay a mixture of rage, despair and determination that wasn't like any of the Holderling's former outbursts. 'To the Jarl.'

'We need some fresh food first.' Birthe leaned forward over the carcass of the deer and began to cut large pieces of meat from the rump.

Ajkell and Hraab had followed the fight anxiously. Hidden in the shadows, they saw how the larger of the two boys fell on the four men pulling the sled. When the first enemy went down, Ajkell had to force himself not to join the fight. Soon he realized that the three were going to win and when the girl with the bow killed the running man with a single shot, he just nodded.

'Nice work,' said he in a whisper.

Hraab looked up at him. 'Why are we hiding? We could have helped them.'

'They are enemies of our enemies.' Ajkell sounded doubtful. 'But are they our friends? I don't know them.' He heard the biggest lad, the fighter, swearing his oath of vengeance. 'Kjelle Almansen? Alman was the Holder here. Is he his son?'

'We'll ask him.' Hraab stuck two dirty fingers in his mouth and gave a shrill whistle.

'Hey!' Ajkell slapped the boy's hand away, but it was too late. The three had turned and stood with their weapons readied.

'Step over here, or I'll put an arrow into your guts,' said the girl.

Ajkell saw her face with the bloody bandage and knew she wasn't bluffing. 'If you're Rannar's enemies, we need to talk,' he said, walking forward with his hands open.

'That's far enough.' Her tony was icy and her bow never wavered. 'Who are you?'

'Ajkell Gudrofsen and the small one here is Hraab. I served the Holderling Meili of Leidwald.' Ajkell felt how tight his face was. 'My master and his young wife were killed when those bastards in the Hold ambushed our wagon.'

'The bridal party,' said the girl.

Ajkell nodded. It had happened on the road hither; of course they'd seen the wreckage. He clenched his jaw. 'I was my master's bodyguard. I failed. We were attacked by bowmen and he caught an arrow in the back. Then I tried to save my lady, but they slaughtered her before my eyes. Someone hit me from behind and when I came to, Hraab was sitting on my chest, trying to rob me. All of the others were dead, to my eternal shame. Now he and I follow Vulf and his men, hoping to kill the murderers. We had lost their trail at first, but yesterday we found them here. The foul deed had been done then. The place is a shambles, but Vulf doesn't seem to care.'

'Vulf?' The smaller of the two lads, wiry and dark-haired, looked at him intently. 'Who is Vulf?'

'He is one of Jarl Rannar's henchmen' said Hraab. 'Coldblooded killer of many, with more blood on his hands than all the monsters in Hella's underworld together. He is the one who did that.' He pointed with his thumb over his shoulder toward Eidungruve.

'Vulf,' repeated the black-haired lad. 'I see. Damn, there are two groups. We met Swinne, who killed the Völva of Belisheim.'

'What?' This shocked Ajkell. Asgisla of Belisheim, counselor of the powerful. 'What is Rannar doing? The King will never accept this.'

'King Vidmer should watch out, Rannar is seeking his throne,' said the girl. 'His man Swinne demanded a prediction of his chances, but my Völva refused. That was why they killed her.'

'Let's not stay here,' said the black-haired lad. 'Once they go searching for those four fools, we've got to be gone.'

'Where to?' said Ajkell.

'To Harkoy. Jarl Dettrich must be warned that Rannar kills under Herigel's colors.'

Ajkell looked at his little companion. The dirty little boy grinned. 'My hawk is just as content with Rannar's blood.'

The bear warrior shook his head. 'The honor of Gudrofsen cries out for retribution. Only Vulf's death can appease its hunger.'

'I am Kjelle,' said the largest of the three grimfaced. 'Holderling of Eidungruve. Those dead are my people. One of them was my father. I, too, thirst for revenge, Ajkell Gudrofsen. However, my duty to Harkoy sends me to my lord. What can we do against Vulf with all his men? We are but three, to die with our revenge unfulfilled serves no purpose. The Jarl will aid us, he has the soldiers.'

Ajkell knew Kjelle was right. He pulled the broken sword from its scabbard. 'This will not be repaired until my honor is restored. Still, I can fight if you need an extra hand.'

The three looked at each other and then the black-haired fellow nodded. 'To defeat Rannar we must have men, so you're welcome, Ajkell.'

'And I?' squeaked Hraab. 'Am I not a man?' The way he held his head and and the crumpled garland on his hair gave him a strange innocence.

The other smiled. 'You too, young one.'

'Let's go then.' Hraab patted the throwing hatchet on his belt. 'She is getting impatient.'

Muus stared at the sled. 'We could use that.'

Birthe looked up from the deer she was cutting up. 'It leaves the tracks. Even a drunken sow could follow us.'

'Not if we go though the Ghestland.'

'Thor!' Kjelle's face was puffy; his eyes red with something like madness shining in them. 'Impossible.'

'We can't go back the way we came. Vulf's men will certainly follow us. We must go through the Ghestland.'

'No! It's hostile.'

Muus shrugged. 'The ghests will stop any pursuers. We just have to be fast and surprise them.'

'What guests?' said Hraab. 'Are we getting visitors?'

'Yes and no.' Muus placed his hands under the edge of the sled. 'All at once, one, two, three.' Together, they got the sled tilted far enough that the remains of the deer carcass slid to the ground. Muus stretched and smiled at Hraab. 'The ghests were once family. Kjelle can tell it better than I, they're his ancestors.'

The Holderling trembled. He gripped his ax in both hands and took a deep breath to steady himself. 'Ghests are undead, like draugar. When my family came here, they built the original longhouse further north, on the edge of some hot springs. After a while, the ground proved unstable. Walls cracked, floors sagged, and cows stopped giving milk. The worst was that the spirits of our buried dead went walking. At last my great-grandfather decided to move his household and they built the present Hold near the silver mine.'

'Nobody goes to the Ghestland anymore,' said Muus. 'But the stories tell that the ghests still roam around, guarding their territory.'

'How wide is the land we have to cross?' said Birthe, while she cleaned the last slab of meat with handfuls of snow.

Muus thought for a moment. 'About five bowshots. All is free of snow and full of warm water creeks. It leads to the mountains bordering the valley. There's a narrow path over the ridge, the Vrakken Pass. Almost nobody knows that the road is there, not even our own people.'

Kjelle stared at him. 'I knew, but how did you?'

Muus sighed. 'You kept me close by, remember? Standing behind you through most of your lessons. I'm not deaf, Holderling.' With a sigh, he dropped the tent on the sled. Then he saw Ajkell's face as he looked at the bundle. 'I'm afraid we took some stuff from your master's wagon. This and a lot of food. I hope you don't mind, but we needed it.'

Pain crossed Ajkell's face. He ran his fingers through his long hair and sighed. 'I don't like it, but I understand the need.'

'Good. Let's go.'

Ajkell took the reins of the sled and they went off the road into the forest.

They hurried on in silence. After an indeterminate time they heard voices yelling in the distance.

They've got our trail,' Ajkell said evenly. 'How far do we have to go?'

Kjelle stared around. 'Half an hour.'

They went on at a trot. Little Búi started to cry, scared by the unexpected shaking. Without slowing, Birthe crooned a lullaby that quieted him. The shouting behind hem seemed closer.

'They don't bother to hide.' Ajkell's voice sounded almost disinterested.

'They think they've got us trapped.' Muus found the thought funny and he smiled. 'We're walking right into the mountains, after all.'

'There.' Kjelle stopped and pointed. In the distance, beyond the trees, was a rocky, snow-free field. 'Ghestland.'

When they came nearer, they saw a moss-grown stretch of land, covered with thin banks of fog from countless steaming pools. To the left were the overgrown remains of the original Eidungruve and straight ahead the mountains beckoned. A hundred or more ghests wandered about, misty patches formed like men, women and children.

Hraab studied them for a while and then he nodded, but he didn't say anything.

Muus raised his hand and they halted. Behind them, the noise of Rannar's men became louder.

'Won't be long before they're here,' said Ajkell, still imperturbable. His hand went to his broken sword.

Kjelle frowned. 'You won't fight with that.' He pulled one of the two axes from his belt. 'Take this; you have to stay alive to fulfill your oath.'

Ajkell hesitated, but then he accepted the weapon. 'Thanks.'

The Holderling stepped onto the snow-cleared land and immediately a ghest hurried towards him. As its transparent arm touched him, the Holderling yelled and jumped back. 'Loki's Cutting Claws, that stings.'

'They don't like us,' piped up little Hraab. 'They're angry at being disturbed.'

'We're not the first to come through this way.' Birthe seemed to listen as she spoke. 'I hear an echo of a chant. Did Eidungruve have a Völva?'

Kjelle and Muus both nodded. 'Siga,' said Muus, thinking of the Wisewoman who had returned to him that useless amulet around his neck.

'She must have sung her party past the ghests.'

'You say people have escaped?' Kjelle grabbed the girl by the shoulder. 'Not everyone is dead?'

With a small shrug, Birthe broke his grip. 'I only know what I said, Holderling. I hear an echo of a chant in the air.' Furrows crept from under the bandage toward her eyes. Then she relaxed. 'It's difficult, but I know how to do the same for us. Trouble is, I've got to follow the earlier tone, to prevent dissonance.'

Muus gave her a sharp look. 'What do you mean?'

'Think of two bards in the same room, both singing different songs. That's dangerous for a chanter; it often brings the opposite of what you want.' She closed her eyes and listened again.

Muus stared at the ghests, who floated around without visible aim. Thin as mist above a quiet lake they were, but more tangible looking than the faceless memories of his youth. He shuddered. His eyes met those of Hraab and the boy winked.

Then, in a clear voice, Birthe began to chant; her half-spoken song sounded harsh and tuneless. She started walking. Without pausing her song, she splashed through the warm water, straight towards the distant mountains. Hurriedly, the others followed, huddling together. The ghests stopped their wandering, gathered and stared at the five living. Birthe sang, repeating her words again and again, while by every step the ghests moved backward. Her voice grew hoarse and sweat ran from her forehead. Muus felt her hand grab his and without thought his other hand went to the skyshard. He felt a tingling flow through his body, from midriff through his arm to Birthe's hand. Now the voice of the girl grew powerful, urgent. The ghests floated aside to let the five pass. For a moment, Birthe's voice faltered and immediately, the ghests surged forward. She regained her song and walked faster. Warm water sloshed around their feet, tree roots made them stumble, but they walked on, surrounded by angry ghests. Then, near the other side, Kjelle stepped in a deeper trench, lost his footing and pitched forward, taking Birthe with him. Her song broke off as she cried out, twisted in mid-air and fell on het face in the water. Búi howled, shocked out of his doze.

Muus grabbed Birthe's hands and dragged her the last feet to the safety of the snowy land. The ghests closed in, while Ajkell plucked Kjelle from the water and carried him out of danger. Hraab waved at the undead. 'Stop, ghests; you're not invited.' Then he laughed, a high, mocking sound, and jumped like a wild-haired frog after the others. 'Hiyaa.' he shouted gleefully, as he landed Ajkell's back. 'I stopped them. I stopped them all.' Búi still yelled in his skins, but quieted as Birthe took him in her arms. Across the streams, a shout rang out. At the edge of the Ghestland men appeared from between the trees.

'Twenty-four,' said Ajkell. 'A third of the whole band.'

'But no Vulf.' There was an unspoken yearning in Hraab's voice.

'No.' Ajkell pulled a face. 'We are too unimportant for him.'

He'll find out.' Hraab held his hands out to Birthe. 'Let me hold him.'

Without a word, the girl handed him Búi and then pointed her wand to the pursuers. 'Put your arms around me,' she told Muus. He obeyed, while the young Völva began a new chant. Now, the tone was demanding and full of menace. A song of robbery and death, with her accusing rod pointing at the men.

A faint wailing rose up. The ghests were in turmoil and turned to the bandits, who had entered the steaming land with visible reluctance. Birthe sang faster and harder, filling their hearts with spirits of war. Almost as one, Kjelle and Ajkell shook their weapons at the pursuers. Little Hraab yelled terrible obscenities. Birthe's accusatory tone swelled; bitter and vengeful. Without a sound, the ghests circled round the bandits. Thick fog rose from the hot water and hid what happened from the onlookers. Muus heard men screaming and the clanging sounds of weapon to weapon; a clamor that slowly died away until all was quiet. The mist lifted and the ghests went back to their aimless wandering. In the warm, bloody streams bobbed twenty-four corpses.

Kjelle stuck his ax in the air. 'I thank you, my ancestors. Eidungruve thanks you. We will never forget.'

Birthe leaned back in Muus' arms, topping him by a head. 'Freya and Freyr, boy.' Her voice was tired. 'Without the strength of the skyshard I couldn't have done it.'

'Was that what I felt? Can you tap that power within me?'

'You did that. I wouldn't know how. You sent the force of the skyshard at me.' She broke away from Muus' grip and turned to face him.

Muus let his arms fall to his sides. 'I didn't do anything. There was a tingle flowing from the shard through my arm to your hand. But it just happened.'

'Then how? Did ... Did the skyshard do it?'

Muus sighed. 'I don't know. If I understood it, I'd feel a lot better.'

'Sorry I stumbled into you,' said Kjelle from behind them. His face was red, but he met the girl's look steadily.

Birthe didn't answer.

'Let's go on.' Muus stared at the snow-capped mountains. 'The farther away we get, the better.'

CHAPTER 8 - TOWER OF PROPHECY

They hurried on and after an hour they reached the foot of the mountains. High above them rose barren slopes too steep to climb.

No wonder that Vulf's men had believed them trapped, Muus thought.

'There is the path.' Relief was clear in Kjelle's voice.

The snow lay piled high and walking was difficult. The path led through two towering mountain walls, broad enough for a small oxcart, and with no more than an ankle-deep layer of snow on the ground. After some hours, Hraab started to lag behind. He never complained, but his face was red from exertion.

'This won't do,' said Ajkell. 'Hop on the sled, lad, let's pull you.'

'How far is it to the top?' asked Birthe.

Kjelle shrugged. 'I don't know.'

'Then you can scout ahead and find out, while we follow more slowly.'

The Holderling gave her an angry glance but he nodded. He looked at Muus and opened his mouth, then he turned and walked away alone. Muus suppressed a grin.

After an hour Kjelle came back, red-faced and short of breath. 'We're near the top. There's a ruin where we can take shelter.'

Birthe wrinkled her brow. 'Is it safe? No wild animals living inside?'

'I haven't inspected it,' said Kjelle stiffly. 'I came back to tell you it's not far.'

'Well done,' said Ajkell, forestalling any more snippy comments. 'We can see about animals when we're there.'

They walked on, in a row, and soon they reached the highest point of the pass. Moon had begun a new journey, drawing pale streaks of light in the snow.

'A tower.' Birthe pointed to a dark spot between the trees. 'Is that your ruin?'

'Yes. It must be Bangerns Torn,' said Kjelle. 'A toll burg from the time the Vrakken Pass was a trade route. I'm surprised it still stands.'

'A toll burg!' Hraab sounded excited. 'Robbing traveling merchants and earning lots of gold.' He stretched the 'o' in gold, so that it sounded like a wolf's howl.

'There wasn't all that much traffic here,' said Kjelle. 'It was more of a robbers' den, from which murdering bastards such as Vulf terrorized the area.'

'Oh,' said the boy. 'That's not funny.'

Kjelle's face was hard. 'No. When I was little, I thought it was an exciting idea. But now ...' He paused. 'One of my forefathers had them all hanged.'

Hraab nodded gravely. 'Good.' Then he yawned. 'I think hanging them was a great idea, too.'

As they approached, they saw a tower of gray stone, with frameless windows and door, but otherwise intact.

Birthe walked to the doorway and peered within. She paused, and listened. Then she sang a few unintelligible lines, and listened again. After a few moments, she turned to the others. 'My song disappeared. The tones should have rebounded, but they just vanished.'

'Is there any danger?' said Muus.

She bit her lip, more uncertain than he had seen her. 'I don't know. My song should have warned me if there was, but I heard nothing.'

'Isn't that good?' said Kjelle. 'If you don't hear anything ...'

Birthe shook her head. 'I should have heard the echo of my song, but I don't. That's weird.'

'We need to sleep.' Ajkell nodded his head to Hraab. 'The kid is dead tired. I suggest we take turns keeping watch.'

It was clear Birthe didn't like the tower, but that she had no valid reason to object. She stepped inside. Muus, bothered by her sense of unease, followed. The starlight through the window holes showed them they were in the guardroom: a semicircular space, with a huge open fireplace to the left and to the right the decaying remains of a table and a few benches. Against the walls were weapon racks for spears and swords. The door to the other half of the ground floor had fallen out of its frame and blocked the passage. Behind it, Muus saw rotting bunks, where the guards once had slept. In the corner stood an iron ladder, near a hole in the ceiling, which gave access to the first floor. It was just a tower; if there was any danger, he couldn't sense it.

Ajkell came in with Hraab in his arms and put him down against the wall, out of the wind. 'He was asleep on his feet; he didn't even wake when I picked him up.'

Muus looked down at the boy. *His hair is like mine.* Black and spiky, stiff with dirt, still with that pathetic wreath of silk flowers askew on his head. He was small, smaller even than Muus. His body was thin as a rat in winter and beneath his rags he was filthy. 'Where did you find him?'

Ajkell arranged his mantle over the sleeping child. 'After the ambush. When I came to, he sat on my chest with a knife in his hands, ready to cut the bronze bracelets from my wrists.'

Muus looked at him in surprise. 'Then you awoke just in time.'

'Yes.' Ajkell's face showed no emotion. 'Hraab is a good kid. Many others else would have put their knife in my groggy throat. He didn't, he was glad to see I still lived. Make no mistake; he is one damn tough boy, for all his size. Vulf's men had murdered his family. He played dead until they were gone and then he followed them; hoping he'd find Vulf alone.'

'And what would he have done then?' Muus was more curious than disbelieving.

'He's an ax thrower,' said Ajkell. 'A rather good one.'

Muus nodded. With a knife or well-sharpened throwing ax, a child could kill an armed adult. If he was lucky.

'He is wise beyond his years,' said Ajkell. 'A lot wiser than me at that age.'

'That's why you are a bear warrior.' Muus grinned. 'You aren't supposed to be wise.'

'And what are you?' Ajkell sat on his heels and stared expressionlessly at Muus.

'A Bryt.'

'And a thrall?' The question came out neutral, as if the answer didn't matter.

There was silence. 'No longer,' said Muus. 'For what I must do, I can't be a slave.'

'What must you do?'

'Have you ever heard of the Shardheld?'

Ajkell nodded. 'Of course, I...' He stopped and stared at Muus. 'You mean you ...' He shook his head. 'Are you a Wiseman, then?'

'I don't know. According to the Völva of Belisheim there's a curse in my head that keeps me from remembering my past.'

'Have you got the skyshard?'

Muus took the pouch from his tunic. A faint blue light crept along Muus' arm and reflected in his eyes.

'Ow enh a bach.' It was Hraab, who sat upright and looked sternly at the blue stone. '*Bach a enh.*' Then he lay down and slept as if nothing had happened.

'What did he say?' asked Muus, while he put the shard back in its pouch.

'No idea. My little brother used to do that. He was telling stories in the middle of the night and next morning he remembered nothing.'

'Even in a foreign language?'

Ajkell looked thoughtful. 'No, not that.'

Muus bent over the boy, but Hraab didn't react. His breathing was even, with faint snoring. 'He's really asleep.'

'You thought he was fooling us?'

Muus sighed. 'So many strange things have happened; I don't know what to think.'

Ajkell studied Muus. He took a deep breath. 'What are you going to do?'

'The Völva told me I must go to Brytanna, to get my memory back. After that, I'll go where Fate leads me. I'll travel to Falrom, probably.'

The bear warrior whistled. 'That's a damned awful purpose, mate.'

Muus nodded and sat for a while, without speaking. Then he went outside.

Kjelle was busy making a fire.

Muus looked around. 'Where is Birthe?'

'She went back a bit,' said Kjelle, while he cut dry splinters from the inside of a fallen branch. 'She wants to make sure that we're not followed and she can hear better without us near, said she.'

'Ah,' said Muus, as he plopped down inside the doorway. 'What a brave Nord warrior our Völva is.' He saw Kjelle's face stiffen, but he was too tired to argue. Muus closed his eyes and leaned his back against the doorframe. It didn't work; whenever he'd doze off, images appeared of flowing fire and glowing stone, heat that hurt him without warming and a sense of urgency that kept him restlessly shifting position.

It was Muus' watch. He sat huddled up by the campfire and tried to stay awake. The night was quiet. No animal moved, nor a branch dropping its load of snow to the ground. Suddenly he stiffened. From the path along which they had come that afternoon, marched two by two a line of soldiers. Without a sound they arrived, their swords and spears at the ready, their faces unrelenting. Muus could only watch, his arms and legs, his tongue wouldn't obey. A moment later he could see the colors of the approaching troop: red and blue. They were Eidungruve's men. He didn't recognize any of them.

At some distance from the tower, the men halted. Their leader stepped forward, a burly warrior in a breastplate, who vaguely resembled Holder Alman in his younger days. A step behind him followed an old man in a gray cloak. The leader in the breastplate opened his mouth and seemed to shout, but there wasn't any sound. The old one beside him stretched his hands out toward the sky. Around his neck he had an amulet that sparked in the darkness. Muus stared hard at it; the amulet looked like the knucklebone he wore. The one that never did anything.

Other warriors emerged from the tower. Ten, fifteen men in leather armor, rushed out to meet the waiting soldiers. From the battlements, arrows shot past Muus and killed two attackers. A tall defender with a white plume on his helmet cheered soundlessly and waved his ax. The attackers stormed forward and now the fight began in earnest, the more horrible for the absolute silence. The battle surged back and forth, while men of both sides fell. The defenders, rough men with ruthless faces, fought like berserkers and soon they seemed to be winning. The old man still stood, with arms raised imploringly, his mouth opening and closing in a silent prayer. Some force must have heard him, because from the night sky a blinding beam of light shot down and hit the top of the tower. For a heartbeat, it was as if rivulets of fire dripped down the walls. Four dark bodies thudded to the ground around Muus and no more arrows were loosed. The defender with the white plume turned around, his face contorted with rage, and his ax split the skull of the old man. This shocked attackers and defenders, and, for a moment, the battle faltered. The man in the breastplate used that moment to swing his own ax and down the plumed warrior. Now the defenders lost all courage. The attackers smelled victory, for their assault intensified. Finally, the last four defenders threw down their arms and surrendered.

The images changed. Now the sky was gray with approaching dawn. It rained hard and water gushed down the five bodies swaying from a nearby beech. The old man lay on his back in the mud, his hands crossed over his chest. Besides the body, the man in the breastplate looked how his soldiers were digging a grave in the soggy earth at the foot of the beech. The soldiers cast furtive glances at the dead Wiseman, as if they were afraid that at any moment a new lightning could explode from his folded hands. They dug in haste, despite the rain, and soon the grave was large enough. The man in the breastplate pointed at two of his soldiers. One of them protested, but a slap in the face made him shut his mouth and, without ceremony, the pair dumped the body of the old man in the hole. Muus stared at the amulet that was still around the Wiseman's neck. Clods of dripping earth fell down on the body and soon the grave was filled. The leader appeared to be making a last speech. He was not addressing his men, though; he motioned to the dangling robbers and pointed to the grave at their feet. It was as if he commanded them to guard the dead Wiseman. Then everything disappeared and the Long Night returned.

'You said you would wake me for my watch,' said an angry voice. 'Were you asleep?' It was Birthe, with Búi in her arms.

Muus shook his head and found his body obeyed him now. 'No, I thought I was dreaming, but I was wide awake.'

Birthe sat beside him. 'Tell me.'

When Muus had finished his tale, she stared motionless in front of her. A look of amazement crossed her face. She hummed a few notes and listened. 'Funny, the tower is empty now, I hear my notes rebound. I don't think it was a dream, Muus.'

'Those soldiers weren't real, nor were the bandits in the tower.'

Birthe thought. 'It was a vision of the past. The vision was in the tower, waiting for someone it could appear to and now it's gone.' She cocked an eye at Muus. 'The soldiers wore Eidungruve's colors?'

Muus nodded. But they were strangers.'

'It could have been the ancestor Kjelle spoke about. He did hang the robbers in this tower.'

Muus looked at the beech across the path. It lacked some branches, but it was unmistakably the same tree. He stood up and walked over. At the spot where he had seen the grave, yellowish grass stems grew above the white. He sank to his knees and brushed the snow away. 'This was the head,' said he, half to himself. Then he drew his dagger and began to dig.

To his surprise, the ground was soft and wet as after a heavy rainstorm. The earth was loose, so he seemed to be opening a freshly dug grave. Prepared for anything, he dug until his knife struck something hard. Moments later he exposed the toothless grin of a skull. With his hand he wiped the earth away. Vertebra appeared, and a piece of collarbone. Suddenly his little finger caught behind a thin silver chain. Carefully he followed the course of the chain until he found what he sought. A finger bone, as small as the one he wore around his neck.

The moment he grabbed it, the chain broke. The bone felt dry in his hand, in spite of the wet earth from where it had come. Muus had expected more, a tingling or some other sign of energy, but there was nothing and he felt a vague disappointment. 'It has a rune on it,' said he as he looked up close at the little bone. 'A different one than on mine. I can't read it.' A sudden movement caught his attention and he looked up. Five translucent shapes, each with a rope around its neck and a weapon in its hand, dropped from the tree. 'Oh Gods.' whispered Muus and he took a step backward with the finger bone clenched in his grip.

Behind him, Birthe began to sing. The draugar hesitated, but one, the leathery remains of a strong warrior with a bald head covered with scars, moved toward him. Muus' hand went to his sword, but he reconsidered. He remembered the old man from his vision. Without knowing what he did, Muus stretched his arms toward the sky. He felt the little bone quiver and a word formed in his head.

F'lach.

His hand seemed to ignite. A lightning bolt shot from the knuckle toward the approaching figure, jumped over to the other four and disappeared. The dead guardians of the grave went out like candles in a storm and Muus groaned. Tears ran down his cheeks while he cradled his burned right hand against his chest.

'Cool it with snow, 'said Birthe through gritted teeth. Her face was red and her eyes flashed. 'You used seidr,' she added in a tone that sounded as if she thought Muus had done something terrible. 'How, I don't know. Male seidr.'

Muus dropped to his knees and stuck his painful hand in a heap of snow. Slowly he felt the pain subside. 'I don't understand,' said he simply. 'I don't know what happened.' With a look at Birthe's face, 'Now you're angry because I used seidr?'

'Yes,' said she. 'Seidr is for women. Males have enough already. What else is left for us? Bearing children?' She spat on the ground and turned her back.

'That was fun,' said a high voice. It was Hraab, who had climbed in the window and looked at them. 'I saw everything. The power of the Shardheld is exciting.'

'The power of the Shardheld,' said the girl without looking. 'You think the skyshard was acting through Muus?'

'Yes,' said Muus quickly. He knew he'd awakened the magic of the finger bone himself in some strange way. But if it'd satisfy Birthe, he'd gladly say the skyshard did it.

'Oh, shit,' said the girl. She shook her head. 'You're lying.' She turned around and wiped the tears from her face. 'And I'm being silly. It was your magic, not the skyshard. The Völva had warned me, knowing my opinion of men. Of the Largassens, the Rannars, who find gold and power more important than friendship and honor. Their kind of assholes I hate, not those few effeminate men who fool around with seidr.'

'You mean me?' said Muus, feeling hurt.

'Of course not.' Birthe gave him an impatient look. 'I mean those Nord weaklings who practice seidr. You manipulate the runes, an art that has nothing to do with us. Not even male Nords use runes that way.' She made an irritated gesture. 'Rune mastery uses the power of the elements. That's male magic. We women have the strength of our songs, weaving the strands of Fate. That's seidr, female magic. Asgisla wanted you to return to Brytanna, because the Druids work rune magic.' She made a face. 'I'm not jealous. Only there are moments I want to smash things, and then such a lightning rune would be nice.'

Muus pulled his numb hand from the snow and started to bend and stretch his fingers. 'It burned. A rune word like that you don't want to speak often.'

'Maybe you should hold it by its chain,' said Hraab brightly. 'Then you won't burn your fingers.'

'Smart kid.' Muus grinned. 'I'll try to remember.'

Hraab stuck his tongue out and fell backward off the windowsill. When Muus lay down beside him, the boy slept again. From outside came the soft hum of Birthe singing as she cradled Búi.

CHAPTER 9 – HELMSHAVEN

'It must have been Eidun,' said Kjelle the next morning. His voice and the glint in his eye betrayed his rage. 'Why would our founding father show himself to you, and not to me, his descendant? You're not a man of Eidungruve, not a Nord, not ...'

Muus heard him in silence, his mind elsewhere.

'It was a vision,' said Birthe, while she breastfed Búi. 'It wasn't about your ancestor at all, Kjelle Almansen. That old Runemaster was the focus.'

'What?' Kjelle avoided looking at her while she had the babe to her breast. *He has seen breasts before, the rabbit. Is he jealous of Búi?* Muus thought absently. Then Birthe's words registered. 'The Runemaster?'

The girl half turned towards him. 'Of course. He left that vision behind for someone who has rune magic. It was a last will. People like him know when they shall die.' Her voice trembled. 'My Völva must have known her death, too. All that time she kept it a secret from me. Freya help me, she knew it.' Leaking tears, she held up Búi until he burped.

Kjelle, only half-convinced, muttered, 'Why all the fuss? Couldn't my forefather have taken that cursed bone?'

Had Birthe been a Runemaster, her glance would have burned the Holderling on the spot. 'What would you have done? That bone caused a deadly lightning. It possessed power that scared the crap out of you and its rightful bearer had just died. Would you have picked it up and put in your pocket?'

The Holderling colored. 'No.'

The girl shrugged. 'Neither did your ancestor. That Runemaster must have known he would not.'

'How could he have had a vision of something that happened after he died?' said Muus.

Birthe looked at him. 'He didn't, the Kalmanir made it for him. The standing stone knows everything that was, is, will and can be. A Völva like Asgisla has the strength to ask for such a vision. Your Runemaster must have done the same.'

Muus looked at his hand and remembered the pain. At least that old one managed not to burn his fingers.

A few hours later, after a meal of toasted bread and venison, they left. Birthe had the lead, with Búi on the sled, asleep in the folds of the tent. The path down from the Vrakken Pass brought them back to King Hurald's Way and from there the rest of the journey went without mishap.

Five times Moon had ridden across the sky when they reached Helmshaven. It was less cold there and the snow lay wet and mushy on the fields. The sky was cloudy over a dark sea and none of it showed the old harbor town in a favorable light.

'It's all just as I remember,' said Muus. He stared at the small huts of salt-bleached wood and thatched roofs, at the muddy and narrow streets where foraging pigs and geese demanded right of way, at the stone quay where longships swayed with the swell, and in spite of himself he shuddered.

'That's a big town,' piped Hraab. 'So many people.'

'About two thousand in summer,' said Birthe with indifference. 'Now it's less, because many merchants have gone south for the winter. You see it at its best; most of the time it's raining, snowing, blowing a gale or all three together. Helmshaven is not a pleasant place to live.'

'Do you know the town?' said Muus.

'I was born here.'

Muus looked at her in surprise. 'You were? I thought your father was a hunter?'

The girl flushed. 'Later he was. When I was small, we lived here in Helmshaven. You see that house in the center, with the shingled roof? That was ours. Now Skid Largassen owns it.'

'It's a big house,' said Ajkell. 'Were you rich folk?'

Birthe nodded. 'My father was Largassen's associate.'

Muus turned and stared at her. 'He was what?'

Again the girl colored. 'Wait! My father had nothing to do with your abduction. He didn't approve of child slavery. For years, my father and Bearjaw went on raids together, cruising up and down the coast of Brytanna, all the way to Espayne and back, bringing home the riches of towns and temples. Slaves too, but never children. It was father's weak spot, Largassen used to say. Then my mother became ill and that summer my father stayed at home. He paid

Bearjaw his share, fifty percent as usual, in exchange for a third of the loot. Largassen sailed, but that autumn he didn't return. Nor did he come the next year and the one after that. My mother's illness grew worse and my father paid for healers, for cures, even for a doctor from Gaul. In the third year, my mother died. My father had spent all the money he had and could loan, and now we were poor. That fall, Largassen returned. He had spent those three years in the kingdom of Duiblinn, raiding Brytanna's west coast, and he returned with his ships laden to the top of the sides with riches. Of course my father went to hear of his adventures and to collect his share of whatever Bearjaw brought home.' She paused and looked at the others. 'Bearjaw didn't *remember* any deals. He denied my father had paid his share. He offered to buy our house for a pittance, 'for old time's sakes'. My father was too tired and certainly too poor to fight a man as rich and successful as Largassen the Viking. He used the money on a good bow and some supplies. Then we left Helmshaven.' She fell silent for a moment. 'This is the first time I come back here.'

'Now we're going to collect gold from that Bear,' said Hraab.

'What?'

'Well, he owes us, doesn't he? He abducted Muus and swindled Birthe's father. He can give us some money to make good.'

'Largassen knows where he found me,' said Muus half to himself. 'I would like him to tell me.'

'Bearjaw won't let you come inside his house.' Birthe took her bow from its case and began to string it. 'He's always been afraid that one of his abducted slaves would come to kill him. One look at you tells him you're a Bryt and then he'll set his servants on you. With me, you will stand a chance. The Viking knows me; I haven't changed all that much and he... liked me.'

'He liked you,' said Muus, the distaste in his voice was palpable. 'Let's go and have a word with this brave Viking.'

'Not all of us,' said Birthe. 'Just you and I; no need to frighten the bastard.'

'And I,' said Hraab. 'It was my idea.'

'All right.' Ajkell looked at Kjelle. 'We frightening ones will wait outside with the sled. Just don't take all day.'

Largassen's house was large for a town dwelling. It had been built with oak on a foundation of stone, with a gallery on all sides, supported by carved columns. The roof, shaped like an upturned longboat, was covered by wooden shingles.

The three stepped inside, straight into the arms of a thin woman in a black and red dress. 'Who are you?' said she, in a voice as sharp as her face. 'The mistress doesn't receive visitors when the Master's a-raiding.'

'Matta,' said Birthe with a smile. 'Is that how I'm welcomed?'

The woman bent her face closer and then her face relaxed. 'Birthe! For Frigga's Love, you're a woman grown. I didn't recognize you, girl; my eyes are failing me. How long it's been? It must be ten years since you left.'

'Nearly,' said Birthe. 'And a lot has happened in them, not all of it good. My father died, and I'm a widow now. So Largassen is away? Who is your mistress?'

'Hilde Luolfsdotter, whom Largassen married two summers ago.'

'Why, the lecherous goat. She's my age and Bearjaw is old enough to be her father and more.'

The woman cackled. 'He likes them young, the Master does. You know that; he liked you, too.'

'I know he did,' said Birthe. 'He wanted to bed me when I was eight. I could've sold myself to him and we'd still be living here. My father didn't want that either, or else I'd have run away. They should've castrated that dog years ago.'

Again old Matta laughed. 'You haven't changed, love. Come; let me take you and your friends to the mistress.'

'Matta was our servant, before Bearjaw took over,' said Birthe. 'She practically raised me.'

Largassen's wife was a small, buxom blonde, with big blue eyes and a child-like expression. 'Birthe.' She stretched her arms out wide and embraced the young Völva with tears in her eyes. 'Oh, I'm so happy to see you, after all those years. Who are your friends?' She looked at Muus and her eyes grew big. 'You... you're a Bryt. Were you a slave? You didn't come to kill him, do you?'

Startled, Muus spread his hands. 'No, I'm not. I wanted some answers.'

'And gold,' said Hraab. 'Don't forget the gold.'

'Hush, child.' Birthe didn't look at the boy, but concentrated on the blonde girl. 'Don't worry; we have come without murderous intent. Why did you marry him, Hilde? Was he such a good match?'

The girl shrugged. 'He's rich. He gives me what I want, and he's often away. When he is home, he has other amusements.'

'Children.' Muus' voice dripped disgust.

The girl looked away, and then nodded. 'He never misuses his own catches; he wants to auction them off as virgins. I have the servants buy some from other traders when he comes home, and when he leaves I sell them again. Oh Birthe, what else am I supposed to do? Should I let him fondle me?'

Birthe stepped back and looked Hilde up and down. 'You've sunk low. If this were known...'

The girl cried out. 'Please don't tell anyone. He'll kill me.'

Hraab stopped wandering through the room and sat himself down on the edge of the table, swinging his bare legs. 'Gold will keep us silent.'

'I'll have you thrown out of the house.'

The little boy grinned. 'Then we'll tell all. And don't try to be nasty, we've armed friends waiting outside.'

Hilde hid her face in her hands. 'You were my friend, Birthe.'

'You're a snake.' Birthe spat on the polished table. 'You leave a bad taste in my mouth, woman. You and that pig Largassen. He ruined my father and stole my friend away from his homeland; he molests slave children and...' She shook her fists at the pale girl. 'You're lucky he isn't home. We need answers, Hilde.' The Völva glanced at Hraab and nodded. 'And some gold would come in handy. We have a long road ahead of us. But the questions come first.'

Muus was already disgusted with the whole thing. The girl had sold her honor for a comfortable life; a cockroach was of more worth than she was. 'I want only one answer,' said he curtly. 'Where did Bearjaw steal me? I must know where I was born.'

The girl gave him a dirty look. 'Kimbel will know. He's my husband's clerk, a slave from your land, Bryt.' She yelled, 'Matta!'

The old servant answered her shrill call. 'You want something?' Her voice sounded surly.

'Find Kimbel; let him bring the trade book.'

A few minutes later an elderly man in a faded tunic entered. He had a large book under his arm. 'Yes, mistress?' There was a strange accent in his voice, which Muus hadn't heard before.

Hilde's glance at Muus was poisonous. 'Ask your question.'

Muus shrugged and turned to Kimbel. 'Largassen stole me away from my home in Brytanna ten years ago. I want to know where this happened.'

The clerk peered at Muus. '*Aogh an'bradh.*'

Muus shook his head. 'I don't understand.'

'You should,' said the clerk. 'You're a Bryt, like me.'

'I'm sorry. All memories from my childhood are gone.'

The man stiffened. 'Ah, it's like that. You must be half-blooded. You're a free man now?'

Muus nodded.

'Good. You should go back. Lemme see.' Slowly he turned the pages. 'Here it is. One boy slave, age six; sold to Hagen of Eidungruve for three gold pieces. Part of the Owwich merchandise. There you have it. You're from Owwich.'

Muus knew he should be glad. It was the information he'd been longing for. Strange; now he knew it left him unmoved. 'Owwich. I can't remember the name.'

The clerk closed the book. 'That's why you should go back. Once in Brytanna, all you knew shall return.' He turned to his mistress. 'Will there be more?'

Hilde waved him away without speaking and Muus felt his cheeks grow hot.

'That's all I wanted to know,' he said and his clear anger made Hilde step back.

Hraab clapped his hands. 'Now, get the gold. Half of everything here belongs to Birthe. So don't be mean.'

A spasm of pain crossed Hilde's face. 'I can't give you much.'

'You don't want to be chased out of town by a mob, do you?' Birthe's eyes were cold as was the tone of her voice. 'Misuse of children, even if they're slaves, is not something a Nord will forgive. It's unmanly and disgusting. 'Give us what you can spare.'

'And then double that,' said Hraab with a wide grin.

Shaking, Hilde went to a large, ironbound chest in a corner. She took a bunch of keys from her belt and opened the lid. After a slight hesitation, she took out a leather pouch and threw it on the table. 'There. Now get lost, all of you. And I hope you'll rot.'

'Probably you will first, after copulating with that filth Largassen.' Birthe snatched the pouch from the table. She checked the contents and nodded. 'That will do. Glad you were sensible, Hilde. I wish you a happy life with your husband.' She marched out of the room, without looking back.

'You humiliated her,' said Matta, waiting for them in the hallway. 'That's good. She's become spoiled meat. Bless the Gods she's stupid, without the servants she'd be sunk and she knows it. I wish you luck, dear.' With that, she disappeared in the house.

Outside, Kjelle and Ajkell turned when they appeared outside. Kjelle looked at Muus. 'How did you fare with Largassen?'

He's away,' said Muus. 'We had words with his wife. After some persuasion, she had Bearjaw's clerk tell me where I was born. And our Hraab blackmailed her to pay us gold for our silence about some of Largassen's habits she betrayed.'

'Not only coins did I get you,' said the boy brightly. 'Look.' From inside his tunic he produced an ivory comb, a silk kerchief, several golden objects and a long chain with precious stones. 'She shouldn't keep these lying around.'

Muus glanced at Birthe. 'Did you see him take these?'

'It wouldn't be much of a trick then,' said the boy and he grinned.

Birthe sighed. 'No, I didn't see a thing. I thought he was next to me the whole time.' She stared at him. 'You're a thief.'

The boy's grin grew. 'It's something to do when times are hard.'

The girl held out her hand. 'They're mine. By your own words, half of Bearjaw's goods are my inheritance.'

Hraab's face fell. 'Loki Poki.' He handed a small load of valuables to Birthe. 'Here, killjoy.'

'Where's that chain? I want them all, or Loki will really poke you.'

The little boy gave her the many-colored neck chain. 'That's the last.'

'Honest?'

'And this ring. That's all, honest.' He sighed. 'Now I'm poor again.' Then his face brightened. 'I can always steal more.'

'No,' said Muus. 'You won't. We've got trouble enough without you setting loads of angry locals on our trail.'

The boy grumbled something inaudible. 'Can I at least steal from the Snake's men? They're after us already.'

Muus laughed. 'You can rob Rannar blind for all I care. As long as you don't get caught.'

'But then you'll come and rescue me. You would come, won't you?' There was an unexpected hint of panic in the boy's eyes and Muus gripped his thin shoulder.

'Of course we would. But try not to, will you?' He turned to Birthe. 'How do we get to Harkoy from here?'

'By ferry boat. Now that we have some money, we can buy passage.'

'Right, let's go'

Tuuri returned to Helmshaven exhausted. He had hardly slept and his stock of food was almost gone. Most of what he had left he'd given to his horse, but it was never enough. The poor girl was like him, hungry and weary, besides having a troublesome shoe on her left rear hoof.

There weren't many folks in the street and most of them walked by without a glance. In the town center, he spied two young men sitting on a sled in front of a tall house.

'Excuse me,' said he. 'Could you point me to a good tavern and a smith?'

The taller of the two shook his head. 'You're out of luck, we're strangers here ourselves.'

'I remember there's an alehouse at the harbor,' said the second one.

'You've been here before?' said the first one in some surprise.

'Last year. I went with Meili to Jonthal, as he went to meet his prospective bride. Of course he knew where the drinks were sold. He had a nose for it.' The young man suddenly looked sad.

'I'll go to the harbor then,' said Tuuri. 'They can point me to a smith, I suppose. Thanks.'

The Ribald Viking was a large barn, no more. A steaming hot common room, where several large fires burned and where large kettles nameless, eternally added to soup simmered. He ordered a large bowl of it with bread and attacked it hungrily.

'Been traveling long?' asked the serving girl, looking him over.

He nodded, sopping his bread in the soup. 'Is there a smith around?'

The girl smiled. ''Course there's one, this is an important town, see. He lives right next door, in fact. That's convenient for business. Aason!' she yelled. 'You're wanted.' A lanky youth entered through a side door.

'Whotsit? Not another leaky pot, I 'ope?'

The girl grinned. 'The lordling's horse needs a reshoe.'

At that, the lad brightened. 'A horse! We don't often get to do that. Is it the pretty one outside, Lord?'

Tuuri smiled. 'She is beautiful, isn't she? Yes, she needs a new shoe left rear. Check the others as well, will you. Do you know where I can buy feed around here? We've come far and she's hungry.'

'I'll see to it, Lord. Love horses an' it would be a pleasure.'

'Great. Call me when you're finished; I'll be staying right here.' Then he stretched out his legs, closed his eyes and slept.

A hand shook him awake and he groaned. 'What is it?'

'Yer horse is shod 'n fed, Lord.' The smith's apprentice smiled. 'Proper lady she is, too. I took the liberty of grooming 'er a little an' she seemed to like it.'

Tuuri laughed at that. 'Oh yes, she's as vain as any girl.' He sat up. 'What day is it?'

The lad looked at him. 'Been away long, have you, Lord? It's the seventh day of the new year. Jest past midnight.'

'Do me a favor,' said Tuuri. 'Go and see if my ship's come in yet. A longship with red sails.'

The apprentice nodded. 'She is, Lord. Came in an hour ago. I seen her before, she must be fast. Still, I like 'orses better.'

Tuuri yawned. 'So do I. How much do I owe you?'

The lad told him and he paid, tipping handsomely.

'Thank-ye, Lord,' said the apprentice with a delighted grin. 'Have a safe journey.'

Outside, Tuuri checked the smith's work and found it well done. 'Well now, girl,' he said, eying her carefully brushed sides. 'The lad did you proud. Let's take you home, before you get used to it.'

He walked her towards Rannar's boat.

'Did all go well?' asked the skipper.

'I delivered my messages,' said Tuuri tiredly.

The skipper grinned. 'You can sleep all you want; you've got a whole week of rest. We're off to Nidros first. The Jarl wants you to check on Lord Brundal; I got some orders for you to deliver. You're finished here?'

'Yes,' said Tuuri. He wanted to get away from the north with its painful memories.

The ferry, an old knarr that had seen better days, landed them on the quay not far from the Jarl's fort. Kjelle, who hadn't known anything but Eidungruve, was impressed. 'So that's what they call a stronghold,' he said. 'I never had an idea, it's big.' He stared at the high, wooden walls seemingly growing from the hill that bore the Jarl's place. Double walls, filled with earth, and with a massive sea-gate, it had an aura of invincibility. Inside, the Jarl's longhouse was easily five times as big as Eidungruve's. With all walls built on a foundation of stone, all visible woodwork carved and the roof shingled with black slate, it underlined the Jarl's power through his wealth as well as through his strength.

At the sea-gate, one of the Jarl's guards stopped them. 'What business have you, friends?'

'I'm Kjelle Almansen, Holderling of Eidungruve. I need to see the Jarl about mine and his affairs.'

The man shifted his stance. 'Then you're out of luck. The Jarl is away at the King's Court.'

'Odin's Beard.' Kjelle felt his face growing red. 'He's away while traitors roam his lands, murdering the innocent?'

''Twas by the King's command he went. If your need is dire, you can speak to Jarl Dettrich's wife Radgundis.'

'The Jarl's wife is conducting his business?' Kjelle couldn't keep the surprise from his voice.

'It's clear you don't know her,' said the warrior with a broad grin. 'The Lady's a former Paladin from the King of Gaul's Court. She has a strong arm and a clear head, Radgundis.'

'Lead us to her,' said Birthe, stepping in front of Kjelle.

The warrior glanced at her. 'And who are you, girl?'

'I'm the Völva Birthe, from Belisheim.' The metal wand in her hand pointed at the gate watcher.

The man paled. 'I meant no offense, Lady.'

'No offense taken. Have someone lead us to the Lady Radgundis; our business can't wait.'

The warrior turned and gave a yell. Moments later a boy of some six years old appeared. 'My son Folki,' said the man proudly. 'Bring the visitors to my Lady, boy, and be quick about it.'

The boy looked at Muus with big eyes. 'You're alves,' said he, as he led them through the gate. 'I know you are; I've seen them before, at night. Dancing in Moon's light. Do you dance in Moon's light?'

'I do,' said Hraab. 'Sometimes, when Moon is full. It's great fun.'

'Is it?' The little boy sounded wistful. 'I dare not go out when they dance; I'm scared they take me with them.'

Hraab nodded. 'That's very smart of you. We alves don't like to be disturbed when we're dancing.'

They entered the longhouse and the boy ran to a tall woman with gray-streaked hair. 'Lady, Lady, I bring you visitors, they're alves.'

The woman smiled at him. 'Alves? My, my. Thank you for bringing them, Folki. Tell your father you've done well.'

'Bye, alves,' cried their little guide as he skipped outside.

'The boy's imagination often runs wild,' said the woman gravely. 'Welcome to our house. I am Radgundis, the Jarl's wife. You came for my husband? I'm afraid the Jarl is away.'

'We bring bad news for his ears, Lady. I'm Kjelle, Holderling of Eidungruve. Great murder has been done there and elsewhere.'

Radgundis' face stilled. 'Follow me to my room. Such things are best spoken of in private.' She led them through the throng of workers dealing out orders left and right, always with a pleasant smile and well received. Once in her room, with the door closed, her face lost its mask of cheerfulness. She looked worried as she motioned them to sit. With a small sigh she sank down on the edge of her bed and got her spindle and distaff out. 'Your pardon, but spinning helps me think. These are trying times. Sometimes it seems there is no end to our troubles. You are Alman's son? I surely haven't seen you at the Jarl's Court before.'

'No, Lady,' said Kjelle. 'I've just passed my manhood's Testing and my father hadn't been well enough to present me yet. I... we come to you as fugitives, with tales of treacherous doings. Murderers stalk the land, ravaging and raping. All evidence points toward a certain infamous Jarl in the south.'

Radgundis fixed her eyes on his face, while her hands never stopped their work. 'Tell me.'

They spoke of the avalanche and Eidungruve's fall, of the ambushed wedding party, the murder of Hraab's family and the sacking of Belisheim. They told of Vulf and Swinne with their false green-and-yellow arrows and at that, the Jarl's lady gasped.

'They're false?' said she, clutching the spindle to her breast. 'They're not Herigel's?'

Muus, surprised at her reaction, shook his head. 'No, Lady. 'Tis all Rannar's doing. He wants to stir up trouble between your husband and Jarl Waldrich.'

'Dettrich must hear of this. He's gone to the King to complain about Herigel. There were other attacks, you see. A farm burned, a Holder assassinated, cattle slaughtered. And with every deed were small things found that pointed at Herigel. We don't want war with Waldrich, the Norden have trouble enough without two Jarls fighting each other. Dettrich went to Nidros to demand the King's support.' For a moment she sank in thought. 'You must go after him, Holderling. You must warn my husband. In the harbor lies a merchant ship bound for the south. Her captain can take you to Nidros.' She unpinned a small brooch on her shoulder. 'Here, take this. My husband knows it well.'

Muus looked at Kjelle. 'It's a step closer to my goal,' said he. 'We'll warn the Jarl, Lady.'

Radgundis clapped her hands and said to the servant who entered, 'Send for Walther, will you, and tell the cooks to prepare a basket of food for the Holderling and his people. They are leaving on the Jarl's business.'

The girl hurried away, while the Lady resumed spinning. 'I hope it won't be too late. So many problems, so suddenly. What is Rannar doing? Surely not...?'

Birthe moved slightly and the Lady looked at her. 'Asgisla knew. Rannar thinks he'd make a better King than Vidmer,' said the girl.

'As if anyone would trust him,' burst out Kjelle.

'More's the pity,' said the Jarl's lady. 'Rannar has abilities. If he weren't such a treacherous hound, he might have won enough support to supplant Vidmer.'

'Might is the word.' At that moment, Búi started to cry and Birthe took him from his skins.

Radgundis looked surprised. 'You have a child with you?'

'My son,' said Birthe. 'The only thing left of an overhasty marriage.'

'Overhasty... you had no father or brother to arrange it?'

Birthe shook her head. 'I have no family, no clan. My father was a Viking and foreswore all our ties on land so he didn't have to share his gains. The old fool.'

At this, Radgundis looked sharply at her. 'I remember you,' said she. 'Your father was Gude, Largassen's partner. My husband and I wondered where you had disappeared to, after your mother died. Is your father gone, too?'

'We lived a hunter's life, till until a bear killed him. He'll be hanging around in Helheim. No Valhalla for Gude Killed-While-Crapping. After his death I joined Asgisla and now I am a Völva, and independent.'

'You're bitter for one so young,' said the Jarl's wife.

Birthe sniffed. 'I haven't been well served by my men. My father exchanged our clan for the Viking's life so that when he was betrayed by the one he trusted most, we had no-one to turn to for aid. The boy I married was killed trying to impress me with prowess he didn't have. No, I'm not proud of them, Lady.'

'At least you're brave,' said Radgundis with a slight smile. 'I'll not offend you by offering unasked-for help, but should you look for fostering, you can always come to me.'

Birthe shook her head. 'Thank you, but no. Búi is mine. I bore him after his father got himself killed and it was my decision not to put him outside in the snow to die, as tradition would have it. I kept him,

fatherless, clanless, carrying my name. His fate and mine are one.'
She frowned for a moment. 'At least until he's grown.'

At that moment, a short man entered. He wasn't a Nord, with his
straight hair cut a hand's breath above the shoulder and his face
clean-shaven. He bowed, something a Nord would never do, and his
words echoed a language from far away. 'You sent for me,
Duchess?'

Radgundis sat straight. 'This is Walther, he is my *procurateur*.
Walther. I want you to bring my visitors on board the *Madgund* and
pay for their passage to Nidros. Tell the ship's Master they're on the
Jarl's business and that he has to sail as soon as the weather permits.'
Then she turned back to Birthe. 'You're a strong girl. May Fate be
with you and little Búi Blue-Eyes.'

Birthe blinked and colored, and for a moment, Kjelle wondered
why. Had she expected censure? He knew well most girls in Birthe's
position would have had the babe dumped in the woods somewhere,
so as not to spoil their chances on a second marriage. He shrugged;
he'd have done the same.

CHAPTER 10 - NIDROS

The *Madgund* was a big ship. With her broad beam and her massive mast, she dominated the local boats as would a whale amidst a shoal of minnows. Her Master was big, too, with grizzled hair that touched his shoulders. Gunthram was his name and he was a Gaul, like Walther and the Jarl's wife, but more of a Nord mariner than the Nords. At least those were his words, accompanied by a hearty laugh. 'No Nord has ever out sailed me, nor will they.'

As soon as the procurator had left the ship, the crew shipped the oars, cast off mooring lines and, careful because of the drifting ice, rowed towards the open sea. Once away from the coast, the sail was hoisted, the helmsman turned the prow of the boat southward and they gathered speed.

The weather stayed calm. There was a lot of ice, both bergs and large floes. The sailors spoke of cold so intense that the sea could freeze overnight and crush your timbers. With nervous hands gripping the wooden rail, the young passengers eyed the glinting ice, their ears filled with tales about the many ships lost and crews drowned in these sluggish waters. But nothing happened. On the second day they left the embrace of the Long Night. Now the sky was gray, snow-laden, with the Sun so low that she touched the horizon. The five rested a lot, huddled together under the after castle, ate the rations the lady Radgundis had provided and kept to themselves. Birthe spent most of her time with Búi, holding him and singing endless songs. Hraab wandered around the ship, always full of questions that the sailors answered with good cheer.

Kjelle sat cross-legged on the deck, polishing his ax and brooding. His father was dead, his home occupied. He had sworn to revenge himself. But how? The familiar feeling of panic started to paralyze him as he realized how unprepared he was to become Holder. Muus had called him a coward. *I'm not a coward,* his mind shouted. *I just don't know what to do.* Muus had been right, when the runt was with him he felt more secure. He stared at his former slave, who sat with his eyes closed on the opposite site of the deck. For years he had hated him. He had hated the way Muus never showed his fear, how he never spoke back or raised his voice in anger as a Nord would do. He had cursed his father for giving him Muus, for rubbing in his contempt for his son by giving him a slave who was so much better at things. But without Muus around, he felt lost. Oh, he could talk the local girls into his bed. And sometimes, he listened when his father spoke with his advisors. Not as often as he'd bluffed to Muus, but he wasn't entirely ignorant. Yet he was hopeless where it counted. He couldn't lead, he couldn't plan and behind his back everybody laughed at him. He cursed softly.

'You're handy with that ax.' Hraab plumped down next to him. The little boy looked at him and in spite of himself, Kjelle smiled.

'I am?'

'Yes. You knocked that hunter of Rannar's out with your ax-handle. That was neat. Could you teach me how to do that?'

Kjelle blinked. Had he done that? The whole fight at Eidungruve was a red haze in his mind. But he did know how to handle weapons. Oskar had seen to that. Oskar, he felt himself go cold thinking of the brute. Cold, cruel and overbearing, the weapon master had been the bane of his childhood. Quickly he pushed the memory away. 'Sure; let's go to the forecastle, I don't want to hit a sailor.' Together, they walked to the small platform on the ship's bow.

'The point is to surprise your enemy,' said Kjelle. 'You can kill your opponent with the edge of your ax, break his skull with the back, or knock him out with the handle. Say you're hacking away at him. All at once you twirl your ax and hit him under the chin with the other end. It surprises the shit out of him. That's one. The other is, you're not striking with the strength of your arm, but with the weight of your weapon plus the swing of your body.'

'Like cutting wood,' said Hraab eagerly.

'Exactly. Trees rarely fight back, but the principle is the same.'

They exercised until the boy began to tire. Kjelle felt more satisfied than he could remember.

That night, he dreamed. He was walking through the snowy forest, alone. Everything around him was silent and his breath formed ice crystals in his face. Then he saw it. A massive bull, shaggy, and crowned with cruel horns. It stood on a small hill, without moving, staring out over its herd. Then, the forest and the bull disappeared. For a moment, he noticed the wind in the rigging and the other sounds of a ship at sea, and then he slept again.

The next morning he had all but forgotten his dream. He spent the hours teaching Hraab all he knew about ax fighting. The boy was a quick study and what he lacked in strength, he made up in agility. He wouldn't be able to knock out his opponent as Kjelle had done at Eidungruve. But his way of jumping on his opponent's chest and planting his imaginary ax in the Holderling´s forehead, proved rather effective, besides a regular source of merriment. Kjelle enjoyed these carefree sessions, and slowly the piggy eyes and the humiliating taunts of his father´s weapon master lost their sting. The third day, Ajkell joined them, quiet and respectful as always. He was a real opponent and Kjelle found himself at times sorely beset. The hardships of the last moons had done wonders for his condition, though, and after a while he noticed that while Ajkell had greater strength, the nature of the bear warrior's fighting was purely offensive. Kjelle found he himself was faster on his feet and through avoidance and a careful defense; he managed to end many of their bouts in a draw. He found a joy in these fights he had never known before and the gray clouds that so often filled his mind had dwindled to almost nothing.

Around noon on the ninth day they sighted the fjord that was the sea entry to Nidros.

'There ye are.' The ship's captain waved an arm towards the narrow strip of water between the towering walls of rock. 'The King's Bite, it's called, because of its teeth. In times of danger, archers are posted on top of the escarpments. Their shooting down on passing ships is a mortal danger. As are the large war machines on the plateau, waiting to lob stones at you. They can sink even a ship like the *Madgund*. It's lucky we come in peace.' He smiled as said he that, but his eyes searched their faces.

Kjelle nodded. 'We're the King's men,' said he. 'We're just bringing a message to our Jarl, nothing more.'

'Fine, I'd like to be able to sail out again without them trying to sink me.' Captain Gunthram laughed his big, hearty laugh, but Kjelle thought he saw some anxiousness in his salt-seamed face. A glance told him that Muus had seen it, too.

'Do you know something of the situation in Nidros?'

Gunthram shrugged. 'I can tell you what I told the Duchess, Holderling. The mood is tense in the capital. King Vidmer is... not popular. I think it's because of the Queen that he's not been deposed yet. Leocastre is well beloved by the people. Nevertheless, those who want the King out of the way are gaining support. The Queen was very worried, last time I was here.'

Kjelle opened his mouth, but Muus was faster. 'When were you here last?'

'A bit over three sevendays ago. I make this trip every month.'

Three sevendays. In that time, everything could have changed. We'd better be cautious. Kjelle turned his head and looked into the fjord. Dark shadows seemed to have gathered there and he shivered.

The first impression Nidros gave was one of strength. The royal castle had been the first stone fortification built in the Norden and looked grim in the snow-pregnant sky.

'Starreborg,' said Captain Gunthram. 'The Queen had it built, after her marriage to Vidmer. She wanted something defensible and that's what it is. Said to be a copy of her brother's castle in Rhemes.'

Kjelle studied the castle. Yes, the captain was right. It looked untakable, with its high, stone walls and the central tower rising over all. He whistled softly and saw Muus looking. 'A difficult place to get into if they don't want you to.'

The Bryt smiled that strange alf-smile of his. 'Let's hope it's not difficult to get out of.'

Kjelle felt his heart flinch. 'Do you think...'

Muus shook his head. 'I don't know.'

'Why are we sailing past?' said Hraab.

The captain smiled. 'Because I'm turning the ship first, youngster. Then I'll moor at the end of the jetty, before that longship with the red sails.'

'With the cable ready to slip?'

Gunthram winked. 'Clever fellow. Where did you learn that expression?'

'From my brother,' said Hraab sadly. 'He wanted to go a-viking, but Pa couldn't spare him at home. He knew a lot of the words, he did.'

'And where is your brother now?'

'Dead. Like Pa and Ma. They were killed in a Fynni raid.'

The captain looked shocked at the boy's statement. Then it dawned on Kjelle what the boy had said. 'Fynni? You mean Vulf's men?'

Hraab's eyes opened wide. 'You hadn't seen? Those funny markings in their faces? They're Fynni from the Ostmark, with Vulf and Swinne as their Tarkynni.'

'How do you know?'

The boy squared his shoulders. 'My father called him that. He knew a lot, my father did. Tarkynn, he called Vulf. "War chief, your face markings show you're of the Fynni. Why do you come here? Why threaten us? Depart with your ulvhednar, go back to your mountains and leave us in peace." That's when the killing started.' A single tear leaked from his eye and Kjelle felt his heart go out to the boy.

'You never told me,' said Ajkell in a soft voice.

'I didn't want to think about it. It... hurts. Here,' the boy thumped his chest.

Kjelle's balled his fists so hard the nails bit in his flesh. Fynni in Dalland. Never before they had come so far to the west. 'Damn you, Rannar.'

'Hush.' The captain looked worried. 'Don't mention that name in Nidros. The King hates him, but should you speak badly of Westhal's Jarl, his many followers in town will find you. Folk have been murdered for less.'

'But we're safely on board. Surely your men are loyal?' said Muus.

Gunthram hesitated. 'Normally I'd put my hand in a fire for them, but nowadays... the Jarl is very free with his silver.'

Kjelle felt himself grow red. 'Thor's Beard.' He lowered his voice. 'So that's why he butchered my people. He wanted the mine. He's going to pay our enemies with our own silver. Dammit, I must stop him. There must be a way.'

Kjelle felt a hand on his arm and he found Birthe looking up at him. 'The Jarl will know what to do. Wait until you've spoken with him.'

The captain spat over the side. 'I don't know what's going on and I'm not certain I want to know. But the Duchess told me to sail you and sail you I will. I'll berth at the end of the jetty and I'll wait a sevendays to return you to Harkoy. After that, you'll have to wait a month for me to return.' Then he hurried off, shouting orders to his men in a mixture of Nordic and Gaullish that Kjelle could barely understand.

Even close-up, the castle was impressive and Kjelle felt his heart beat faster as they walked towards the gatehouse. Through it, he saw the double drawbridge over the narrow gorge that separated the castle from the mainland and he whistled softly. Truly an impregnable place.

'Halt.' A hirdman, one of the King's own warriors, barred their way. 'Who are you and what do you want?'

Kjelle was surprised by the hostile tone in the man's voice and the way he held his spear. 'I'm Kjelle Almansen, Holderling of Eidungruve. I seek Jarl Dettrich with a message.'

The soldier seemed to tense and he looked at his mate. 'Jarl Dettrich, eh? Follow me inside, Holderling.'

Something inside Kjelle cried, *Watch out, danger.* He squared his shoulders and followed the hirdman over the bridges to the closed main door. As they neared, the door swung open and they came to a small courtyard in front of the rock that carried the towering keep. A narrow path ended at the wooden ladder to the first floor. Kjelle, used to get into the simple longhouses. How could a lord, a King, distance himself so far from his people?

They entered a circular room, with a large fire burning at the other side from the door. In front of it was a high seat, empty.

The hirdman led them through the crowded room to the fire, where a richly clad man stood warming his hands. He saluted. 'Jarl Brundal, these people walked up to the gate house, asking for Dettrich.'

Slowly, the Jarl turned around. 'Did they now?' Kjelle felt his stomach turn as he saw the calculating eyes of the man staring at him. Brundal, the Marshall of the Court, foremost advisor to the King, had a nasty reputation. A proud, greedy and violent man he was said to be.

'Who are you?'

Kjelle stood straight. 'I am Kjelle Almansen, Holderling of Eidungruve.'

'Eidungruve... A Dalland man.' Brundal was silent for a moment. Then he snapped: 'What do you seek here?'

'I bring a message for my Jarl,' said Kjelle 'His good wife sent me hither.'

'His good wife.' Brundal gave a laugh. 'Dettrich is a traitor.' Suddenly he shouted. 'Dettrich killed the King. He is a dishonorable dog and shall be hunted until he's killed like a dog.' He turned to the hirdman. 'Lock them up. They will be interrogated when Jarl Rannar arrives and then trice-killed. The Gods will be grateful for some fresh offers.'

Kjelle opened his mouth, but no sound came. Helplessly he glanced at the others, but found no answer there.'

The hirdman turned around and shouted a command. Immediately a handful of armed men hurried forward to join him. Then he looked at Kjelle. 'Follow me.'

Kjelle looked around and saw the stares of the people in the room. Some were openly hostile; others only curious, but no-one questioned Brundal's command and he realized there wasn't any help to be had either.

Tuuri stood in the shadows of the throne room, waiting until Jarl Brundal recognized his presence. For two days he'd stood there, for two days the Landesregent had kept him dangling. He thought of the great news waiting for him when he arrived in Nidros. King Vidmer was dead and Brundal, who was firmly Rannar's man, had taken over. Then why wouldn't the Regent receive him? Every time he was fobbed off with arguments like 'too busy with the change of leadership' or 'the volatility of the situation', while Brundal hung around in the throne room and didn't seem to be doing anything.

The doors opened and like everyone else he craned his neck to see who entered. It was a group of five young people, and seeing them, he involuntarily stepped back deeper into the shadows. *They're the two fellows from Helmshaven. The others...* His breathing stopped and his heart changed to ice in his breast. *It can't be! He's dead. He must be dead.* It was the dying boy from Vulf's raid. The smallest one, the one he'd lied about to Vulf. There wasn't any possible doubt; it was him. Somehow, he must have escaped the flames, recovered from his wounds and met up with the others. He couldn't hear what Brundal was saying, but it was clear the five hadn't expected it. Then he heard Brundal shout something about Jarl Dettrich being a traitor and shortly afterwards the five were arrested and marched away.

Tuuri let out a sigh of relief. The child hadn't seen him. What had they wanted? Whatever it was, it had brought them great danger. Being close to Dettrich was as good as a death sentence.

The side door to the throne room flew open, a boy of some twelve winters marched in, his face set, and his fists balled. *Prince Ottil!*

'I want an explanation, Lord Brundal,' said the boy in a clear voice. 'Why are my orders ignored? Why am I kept in ignorance about my father's murder?'

'Prince Ottil,' began the Landesregent, but the boy cut him short.

'I don't want excuses, Brundal, I demand an answer.'

Brundal stiffened. 'You can't demand anything; you're nothing but a stripling. I rule in King Vidmer's place.'

'Then you're a cursed usurper, Brundal,' snapped the boy.

'Enough! Guards, take His Royal Highness to his apartments and lock the doors. I need no little boys running around in my throne room.' There was some murmuring at that, but an angry glare of the Landesregent silenced it.

'You can't do this!' The boy was white with fury. 'I'm to be King now.' But guards came and half-dragged the young Prince away. Again, there were sounds of protest.

'Silence!' Red-faced, Brundal confronted the courtiers. 'The Prince will be well cared for, but he's only a child. An unruly child. There is a new order now. Jarl Rannar is on his way here and he'll decide how the future will be. Until he is here, the Prince will remain in his rooms. You may all leave.'

Tuuri was about to obey, when he heard Brundal's yell. 'Not you, messenger. Come here.'

Brundal paced back and forth, his face furious and uncertain at the same time. Tuuri stood and waited patiently. After some minutes, Brundal halted. 'I have kept you waiting, I'm sorry. Any orders you carry are superseded, Master Tuuri. Lord Rannar is coming. It will take at least a week before he is here and I fear for the Prince's safety. You saw his impudent behavior, his childish tantrum, and you'll know them for the same foolishness his father was infamous for. Still, I'm afraid somebody will try and get the Prince out of our hands. I can't allow that. Nor can I do anything to the brat without Lord Rannar's permission. I've one option left. You will take the Prince and his tutor to Lord Rannar. Let him take care of the child, and I can handle the situation here. Clear?'

Tuuri, dumbstruck, nodded.

'Well then, return to your ship. I will have the Prince and his tame paladin brought to you soon after midnight. You sail at once and take the boy off my hands. Lord Rannar will be in Agdir when you arrive. Call him the Warlord. On no account use his name.'

Tuuri bowed. He hadn't thought about this, while dreaming of Vidmer's deposition. He barely knew there'd been an heir and apparently a brave one. Of course the boy resented Brundal's takeover. 'Yes, Lord,' he said. 'I'll return to my ship then.'

As in a dream, he walked back to the harbor. Carrying a boy Prince into exile wasn't a noble deed. *Not into exile, into safety*, he thought. That sounded much better.

The soldiers hurried them away, out of the great hall.

'The King was killed?' said Kjelle once they were outside.

The hirdman glanced at him. 'Three days ago. He choked on a horn of wine. Poison swelled his throat shut, the healers said. Dettrich was with him, and nobody else. In the confusion, he and his men fled. What more evidence of his guilt do you need?'

'Or of his sense of caution perhaps?' said Muus. 'Had he stayed, wouldn't they have named him murderer still, just as we were judged without any evidence at all?'

'Shut up,' growled one of the soldiers and prodded Muus' shoulder ungently with the blunt point of his spear.

In silence, the soldiers herded them down the rocky path, to a door at the bottom. The hirdman beat on the wood with his sword hilt and the door opened from the inside. A small man with a pinched face shone a lantern at them. 'New visitors?'

The hirdman nodded. 'They're to be kept here till Jarl Rannar calls for them. So feed them sometimes.'

The smell of sweat and decay in the narrow corridor made Kjelle gag.

'Go on,' said the soldier. 'Your room waits at the end, noble Holderling.'

Kjelle colored hotly at the tone in his voice. That was Oskar's voice. The same taunting he had endured for so long. 'Don't use that tone with me, you low born goat.'

The warrior grew pale. 'Goat? Why, you beardless monkey!' He raised his spear and knocked Kjelle against the wall. Blood spurted from the Holderling's nose and mouth. Again, the man swung his spear, but now Ajkell gripped the shaft.

'No more, soldier of the King.'

The man exclaimed and tried to wrest his spear from the bear warrior's grip. But Ajkell pressed the weapon down, forcing the soldier to his knees, and pushed. The man lost his balance and fell in a heap. With a curse he scrambled to his feet and went for his sword.

'Enough.' said the hirdman. 'Remember Brundal's words, Rannar wishes to see them. Alive. Now act like a soldier.'

The second man sheathed his sword and picked up his spear. He didn't speak, but his eyes yelled his wrath.

Kjelle wiped the blood from his face. 'Rannar may hang me, stab me and drown me, but I am Holderling and a kingsman. I will report your behavior to the Jarl, soldier.'

The corridor ended at a door. 'Your cell,' said the hirdman. 'It's dark and unfitting, but perhaps Jarl Rannar will set all aright. He's said to be a fair man.'

'We've got to take their weapons,' said the soldier sullenly.

'No. Time enough for that when it's necessary. For now we'll leave them with their honor intact.'

The jailer lifted the bar and opened the door. 'Here ye are. Not the best beds in town, but the best I can offer.'

Hard hands pushed them inside, the door slammed shut and the sound of the key in the lock was like the closing of the doors of Helheim.

'Come here with your face,' said Birthe. 'Let me feel if there's any damage.'

A blue glow lit up the cell and Kjelle cursed. 'That damned stone again.' Speaking was difficult, his lip felt twice as thick as it ought.

'But its light helps.' From one of the satchels on her belt she took a dried leaf. 'Here, press this to your lip. It will sting, but it prevents your mouth swelling shut.'

Hastily, Kjelle held the leaf to his lower lip. Unbidden tears sprang to his eyes, but he forced them back.

'You were brave,' said Hraab, 'talking back to that soldier.'

'Foolish-brave. The men could've killed you and then what?' Birthe let go of Kjelle's nose. 'The bleeding has stopped.'

'Not foolish,' said Ajkell. 'A soldier of the royal guard using that tone to a kingsman is unforgivable. The Holderling couldn't have done anything else apart from splitting his skull. And that would've killed us all.'

'Men,' said Birthe bitterly.

Ajkell shrugged. 'I'm sorry, Völva, but that's the way it is.'

The girl looked at him, but she didn't say anything.

'We must get out of here,' said Kjelle. 'I refuse to be slaughtered '

'Getting out is easy.' Hraab put a finger on the door. 'This lock is easy to pick. I could get it open with me eyes shut.'

'Well, what are you waiting for?' Kjelle stepped forward. 'We must get away.'

'Not so fast,' Muus had been silent for a while, and now his words halted the Holderling.

'What?'

'Getting past that door is one thing, but how do we get out of the castle and over those bridges?'

Kjelle turned. A feeling of complete hopelessness came over him. 'You're right.'

'I can spy around.' Hraab looked eager as always, his eyes glinting. 'I'll slip by that jailer; I bet he spends his days drinking. Once outside, I'm only a kid. Not a big 'un like you. Nobody will notice me.'

'It's too dangerous,' said Muus.

'No more dangerous than waiting for Rannar.' Ajkell looked at the little boy. 'I say let him try.'

'Woohee,' the boy yelled, but softly. From the folds of his tunic he drew a thin knife. Humming an unfamiliar song, he started picking the lock. His hands, always fluttering like busy bees, were rock-still, controlled. A click sounded, and he sat back on his knees, looking around. When he had everyone's attention, he pushed the door open and peered into the corridor. Then, with a cheery smile and a wave, he slipped out.

Kjelle let out his breath. His eyes met Ajkell's, who gave a slight nod, and then shrugged.

CHAPTER 11 - RUNEMASTER

It took some time for Hraab to return, time the others spent sleeping, while Birthe fed Búi and Muus sat staring at a spot on the wall where water leaked inside. Drip, drip, drip. The rhythm was blue in his head: water-blue, sky-blue. The skyshard filled his head, his being. A sea of blue; he only had to jump and all would be well. The sea rose, over the jetty in the harbor, over the stone quay, into the streets. It drowned the houses, the people, and the soldiers; crashed down the doors of the dungeon and gently brought him out, free. Free on board the waiting ship, free to go south, to Falrom, to... No. Not that way. Too many people would die, innocent people, friends. The skyshard burned on his chest. Images of tornadoes whirled past, bringing destruction, hail, fire, creating cover for them to escape. No. Not like that either. A hand shook his arm.

'Wake up. We're getting visitors. Put the stone away.' Muus opened his eyes and the warmth of the skyshard disappeared as he looked at Hraab.

'You're back.' Hastily he put the skyshard back in its pouch.

The boy grinned. ''Course I am. But wake up, there are people coming.'

'What kind of people? Soldiers?'

'Those, too. They're with someone important and two others. I don't know them, but they move with stealth. Quick, there they are.'

Outside the cell, keys jingled and then the door swing open. An older man stepped in. His hair was gray; his face lined and full of sorrow. He stopped in the middle of the cell and looked them over. What he saw seemed to reassure him, for he relaxed and closed the door behind him.

'Which one of you is the Holderling of Eidungruve?'

Kjelle brought his hand to his heart. 'I am, Kjelle Almansen.'

The stranger nodded. 'Welcome to Nidros. What was your business here at court?'

'I had a message to my Jarl, Dettrich of Dalland.'

'You walked up to the main gate and boldly asked for Dettrich, knowing he had committed regicide and fled like a coward. Why?'

'I didn't know anything about the King's death,' said Kjelle. 'We had just arrived over sea and went directly to the castle.'

The stranger pulled his lip. 'You came over sea. What ship?'

'The *Madgund*.'

'Yes, I saw her arrive. 'She's a familiar sight in Nidros. What is your message?'

Kjelle hesitated. 'It was meant for my Jarl's ear.'

The man raised his brows. 'Would you keep it a secret from the King?'

'Of course not,' said Kjelle. 'But the King is dead.'

'I am Logmar, King's Lendmann and Councilor. I speak with his voice.'

'Tell him,' said Muus and he saw the Lendmann turning his gaze upon him.

Kjelle sighed. Once more, he told everything, passing over the skyshard. He stressed the importance of the arrow feathers, emphasizing the part Rannar of Westhal played. While he spoke, Logmar's face became even more strained.

'This is bad,' said he when Kjelle had finished. 'Eidungruve's mine taken, Asgisla dead, Herigel's colors misused. Now the King lies murdered and Rannar is on his way hither.'

'To take the Crown,' said Birthe.

The councilor looked at her in surprise. 'You think he would be brazen enough to supplant Prince Ottil? I'd suppose he wanted the Regency and become the power behind the throne.'

'He sent one of his men to my Lady Asgisla, wanting to know his chance of success in supplanting Vidmer. I was there when the question was asked.'

Logmar eyed her doubtfully. 'You were there? Who are you then, my girl?'

Birthe took the wand from her belt. 'I was Asgisla's pupil, Birthe of the völur.'

'You name yourself Völva? That's quite a claim for one so young.'

'Asgisla named me so, after I had passed all her tests.'

'Then I must accept what you say. Damn that Rannar for a vile scoundrel!' He turned to Kjelle. 'You have gathered a remarkable company, Holderling. A Völva, two Bryts, a bear warrior.'

Muus felt the skyshard move and before he knew it, he had taken it out. Blue light filled the cell and the Lendmann gaped.

'More strange than you think, Lendmann Logmar. I am Muus of Owwich, the Shardheld.'

'Gods.' Logmar had paled. 'A new shard has come?' He turned to Kjelle. 'I'll escort you and your people to your ship. I ask one favor: that you take two others with you. They, too, have urgent need to escape from Nidros.'

Kjelle nodded. 'Agreed.'

The Lendmann clapped his hand to the small sword at his side. 'Follow me.'

Once outside, Muus saw it was already dark. Moon had hidden himself behind the clouds and the wind was cold. Surrounded by the soldiers they hurried through the narrow streets of the town, until they came to the jetty. In the distance, they saw the port light of the *Madgund* winking. As their feet touched the wooden floor of the jetty, six shadows stepped forward from the dark.

'Halt. This place is out of bounds.'

'Not for me, hirdman,' said Logmar.

'I'm afraid even for you, Lendmann. Orders of the Landesregent.'

'Brundal can't order me, hirdman.' Logmar gave a curt command to his soldiers, who formed a barrier across the jetty. Then he turned to Kjelle. 'Run to the ship and get out of here. Fast. These are the two I spoke of, they'll join you.' Two persons, cloaked and unrecognizable, stepped from amidst the soldiers. One was tall as Kjelle, the other small as Hraab. 'Now run.'

'My bowmen will have to shoot them, Lendmann.'

'Hirdman, I'll see you dead first.'

Without a word, Kjelle ran, Muus on his heels and Birthe with little Búi bouncing on her back. Ajkell followed with the taller of the two strangers. The small cloak and Hraab after a few steps seemed interested in making a race of it and they darted forward.

From behind them came sounds of fighting. For a moment, the taller cloak stumbled, but then they ran on, with an arrow protruding from the stranger's left arm. The jetty was long, 150 feet at least, Muus thought, and empty of ships but the red-sailed longboat. Then he stopped thinking and just ran. As they neared the *Madgund*, he heard captain Gunthram's voice shouting commands. Horny hands hoisted the main sail, the gangway ran out and they dashed on board, Hraab first, and the small cloak a close second.

'Cast off,' sang Hraab as he waved at the captain, 'cast off for the open sea.'

The captain didn't need any encouragement. 'Slip the lines.'

The *Madgund*, catching the wind, gathered speed and they were off.

'We have made it.' Kjelle's face was flushed with relief.'

'We're not free yet.' The captain scanned the top of the escarpments on both sides. 'There.' He pointed to the left and the still panting fugitives saw a mounted figure galloping. 'The messenger's going to alert the artillery at the mouth.' He watched the hurrying horse for a moment. Then he sniffed the wind and shook his head. 'We're not going fast enough.'

'Captain.' The voice of the sailor sounded strained and they all turned towards him. Behind them, the Moon stared through a rent in the clouds and in his light, they saw two sleek galleys coming round the bend in the fjord.

'Out oars' cried the Captain across the ship. 'Every bit of speed counts. They're King's ships. You really got them stirred up. What did you do to the King?'

'The King is dead,' said Kjelle. 'He was murdered three days ago. Rannar's puppets are in charge now.'

Gunthram cursed. 'So it's happened. Rebellion. Well, we can discuss all this later. If there is a later.'

Slowly, the horseman on the escarpment drew ahead of the ship and just as slowly the two longboats gained. Time and again the captain sent his men to trim the sail or shift some cargo to coax all the speed out the *Madgund*.

Finally the mouth of the fjord came into view. The King's Bite had seemed small when they entered but appeared no more than a mouse hole now. Without warning, a fountain of salt water rose alongside the ship and drenched the hurrying sailors.

'That was close,' said the captain. 'Let's hope it was luck.'

Behind them, the longboats were near and arrows bit into the deck. A sailor screamed, and pitched forward, a long shaft protruding from his back.

'Surrender.' a voice cried from the dark. 'Return the Prince unharmed, or by Thor, we'll sink you.'

'The Prince?' roared the captain. 'What are you talking about?'

'He's talking about me,' said a boy's voice and the small newcomer shrugged off his cloak. 'I'm Prince Ottil Vidmersen. They don't want me back, they want to kill me.'

'By the Gods.' Before the captain could say more, a second flight of arrows made holes in his sail.

Muus felt his hands tingle and the skyshard on his breast grew warm. He stared at the Prince, a sturdy lad about Hraab's age, with long hair and a promise of strength in him.

The boy's eyes glittered and the lines in his young face pronounced not fear but a terrible anger. 'I need to go to my mother, Captain. You are to take me there.'

Gunthram wiped his sweaty brow; the fear was on his face now. 'What a dirty trick.' He turned to Kjelle. 'Did you know? Having him on board is a death warrant for all of us.'

'Even more reason to fight, captain.' Muus flexed his fingers as the itching grew.

The captain took a deep breath and regained his color. 'Your pardon, Prince. You're my Queen's son and I'll defend you with my life. Though what remains of it will be brief, I fear.'

A second splash proved that the men with the catapult weren't amateurs.

'The next one will hole us,' said Gunthram. An arrow hit the helmsman behind him and the ship started to swing. With an oath the captain sprang to take his place. More arrows flashed past and another seaman died.

On impulse, Muus took the lightning rune in his right hand and put his left over the skyshard on his breast. Blue light engulfed him as he, holding the rune high, called *F'lach*. The result was immediate. Lightning flashed down from the sky, exploded the catapult on the escarpment, sprang over to the two longboats, turning them into flaming horror, and sent a shower of sparks over the heeling *Madgund*. Fires started on board, smoke came from the sail, and Muus screamed in agony as he burned. Then, everything went black.

From the deck of the red-sailed ship Tuuri had witnessed it all. He'd watched Logmar's confrontation with the guards, he'd seen a group of persons running pell-mell to the big vessel moored ahead of them and as the merchantman took off, he heard a soldier on the jetty curse. 'They got the Prince!' He turned to the captain. 'After them.'

Two large war galleys slid past them, drums beating and rowers trying to make their best speed. The galleys rounded the bend before Tuuri's longship parted the jetty.

'I'll keep my distance from those boys,' said the skipper. 'They play rough and I'm not built for that.'

With the maw of the fjord in sight, sudden holes appeared in the merchantman's sails.

Tuuri gaped and the skipper pointed to the top of the escarpment. 'Artillery,' he said. 'This place is well defended.'

The two war galleys shot a volley of arrows and from on high a new load of stone hit the merchantman.

'They'll sink her,' said Tuuri. Then he froze. Lightning flashed down from the clear sky. It hit the top of the escarpment and the stone throwers exploded into splinters and pieces.

'Down the sail!' shouted the skipper. 'Rowers back up, back up!' Slowly the longship started to move in the opposite direction, while Tuuri stared at the display of lightning now hitting the war galleys. Sailors and archers on the two ships tumbled, smoking, and many jumped over board to douse their flaming clothes. The sails started to burn and crashed down into the wooden hulks. Then, without fuss, both boats disappeared into the deep waters.

Tuuri stood looking after the merchantman, sailing on as if nothing had happened. 'After them,' he said finally.

The skipper shook his head. 'We've got to pick up the survivors first.'

Tuuri nodded. He looked at the bobbing heads and waving arms. 'How many men did they carry?'

'Sixty each,' said the skipper. 'The best trained men of the Fleet.'

They picked up eight living sailors. Living in body, for most of them had lost their minds. The sudden counter-attack, just as they thought the chase completed, the merciless lightning against which there was no defense, had terrified even the hardest of them out of their wits. Many were terribly burned and the stink of scarred flesh filled the ship. Back in Nidros the soldiers who came to collect the survivors, whispered a tale Tuuri hadn't heard before. 'Shardheld,' they muttered. 'He said it himself, told Logmar he was Runemaster and Shardheld. A blue light sprang from his body. What evil luck!'

'We had more luck than you think,' said a hirdman sharply. 'He could've burned the town but he didn't. He only killed those who tried to kill him.'

'They called out that Prince Ottil was with them,' said a man from Tuuri's ship. 'Why did we try to kill our Prince? He's a good lad.'

The hirdman glanced at Tuuri and recognized him as Rannar's man. 'Shut up, you fool,' he said to the sailor. 'Bring that body ashore.'

Tuuri turned away from the blackened man, who must have died on the way back. Kill the Prince? Who ordered that? The master wants him alive and well. Damn, he should hurry north, before his whole plan goes to the dogs. And what is a Shardheld? 'Can we sail now?' he yelled to the captain. 'I must report this whole shambles to Lord Rannar.'

The captain whistled sharply and as the big sail rose in the mast, the last man on the quay took a spurt and jumped on deck. 'We're off, Messenger.'

'Fast as you can,' snapped Tuuri, angrier than he'd been for a long time. 'Lord Rannar will flay us all if we tarry.'

CHAPTER 12 - CHANGES

Muus awoke in a sea of pain. His hands, his chest burned as if on fire. Bitter smoke clung to his nostrils and nausea fought with a terrible headache. He wanted to die.

'I told him.' That was Hraab's voice, sounding aggrieved. 'I told him to hold it by the string. But would he listen? No. Stubborn fool.'

'He looks like roast beef,' said another young voice. 'Is he going to die?'

'No, he ain't. The skyshard won't let him.'

'What is that skyshard? I must have it, it's powerful.'

'You can't have it, egghead. It's too powerful for a Prince. It's going to save the world.'

'But...'

A female voice interrupted. 'That's enough, Prince. You're bothering the Shardheld while he needs to rest. On deck with you both.' She sighed. 'Ottil's as blunt as a sledge hammer, just like his mother. He's got her brains and willpower, and the muscles of his father.'

'A powerful combination.' said Birthe.

'Yes, but it taxes my patience. What next?'

'I'll do the Song of Skylbjear.'

'I don't know that one, so I'll do the salve.'

'It draws on Freya's wisdom.' Then she started to sing and Muus drifted away.

When he awoke again, the pain was at dull ache, but bearable.

'You're awake?'

Muus opened his eyes and stared at Kjelle's face. He was surprised at the concern. 'Where are we?'

'At sea, two days out of Nidros. You saved us, you know. You sank the longboats.'

'Did I? It hurt.'

'I believe it; your body looked like well-cooked meat. What happened?'

'Don't know. I named the rune, and then the lightning... and somehow, it burned me, too. Who was that woman?'

'She's a paladin, from Gaul; she's the tutor of the Prince.'

'Then there really was a Prince? I thought I'd dreamed that.'

'He's real enough. Proper little berserker, too, is Prince Ottil. Not like I was at that age.'

Muus heard the bitterness in his voice. 'You're doing all right now,' said he. 'You haven't panicked once since Eidungruve.'

'I can't afford to. I must avenge my people. I know I'll die trying, so there is nothing else to be afraid of.' For a moment he was silent. 'Aren't you ever scared?'

Muus thought for a moment. 'I don't feel much emotion, these days. No fear, no hate. I do what I must.'

'It's strange,' said Kjelle. 'I've hated you for ages, but no longer. I know now that I really hated myself. Because of my father, because of that bastard weapon master.'

'That drunken sot? I never understood your fear of him. All bluster, no bite.'

Kjelle was silent. 'The weapon master shouted all the time and humiliated me. I never saw him as a drunkard. Nightmares he gave me.' Then he laughed. 'A drunken sot. That's all he was. Thanks, I hope you think a bit better of me, now.'

Muus patted the Holderling's arm. 'Don't worry. I understand how it was. You'll make a good Holder, Kjelle, just like Siga predicted.'

'Siga?' Kjelle sounded surprised. 'Did she say that?'

'She said you'd be a good leader, if you'd get more confidence in yourself. She was right. Now, help me up, will you? I need some fresh air.'

With Kjelle's arm in his back his wobbly legs carried him on deck. As he appeared, blinking in the clear sunlight, the sailors cheered.

'Why is that?' Muus said, surprised.

Kjelle smiled. 'I said you saved us. Without your lightning, they would have sunk us. The men are grateful.'

'Welcome back.' The captain gripped Muus' arm in a respectful way. 'My apologies, I never realized what a powerful Runemaster you are. You cooked their goose most properly.'

'Myself, too,' said Muus ruefully. 'Where are we?'

'Halfway to Agdir; we just passed the port of Bjergvin.'

'Agdir? What are we going to do there?'

Kjelle coughed. 'It's near Ejrikastelle, where the Queen resides. Ottil needs to join her now his father is dead.'

Muus looked around. 'Where is the Prince?'

'He's with Hraab on the forecastle. Talking. I thought girls talked a lot, but young boys are just as bad.'

Muus turned around as he heard Birthe call his name and joined her at the railing. With her was a tall young woman in a mail coat. Even here she wore a costly steel helmet and on her back a tall sword. She was pretty, thought Muus, though in a cold way.

'You're up and about,' said Birthe. 'That's good. The paladin and I have sung ourselves hoarse over you.'

'We did,' said the paladin. Her voice was as Muus remembered, light and stern. 'But it was a good deed, for you are a servant of the Gods as much as the Völva and I.'

'I am?' For a moment, Muus felt confused.

'Of course. The Shardheld is selected by the Gods themselves, to do their will.'

Muus saw the laughter in Birthe's eyes, but he nodded gravely. 'I see. Well, I must thank you for your part in my recovery. May I ask your name?'

The paladin bowed slightly, a curious gesture in the eyes of one who had grown up among egalitarian Nords. 'I am Valiantrude de Vergy, Paladin of the Court in the retinue of Queen Leocastre of the Norden, and tutor to Prince Ottil, her son. You need not thank me, thank the Gods for their aid, your burns were extensive. That lightning must have grazed you. The skin on your upper body and your arms was red and blistered. But the skyshard itself must have helped our singing and the salves we gave you, for the blisters healed fast.'

'The wound on your head has healed as well,' said Muus. 'There's hardly any scar visible.'

Birthe colored. 'It was a side effect of your healing. Valiantrude caught an arrow in her upper arm during our dash for the ship. That wound is gone too.'

'The Gods are merciful.' The paladin bowed and made Odin's sign. Muus thought of the skyshard and the terrible lightning. *Not the Gods, it was the shard. Avalanche-maker, Lightning-bringer.* He suppressed a shudder.

Two days later around noon, a young voice shouted from the mast: 'I can see the Nez.'

The paladin clenched her fists and looked up with deep disapproval on her face. 'The Prince is with the look-out. He was supposed to be at his studies. I should have known better.'

Muus smiled. 'See it as an exercise in leadership. The sailors love things like that and it enhances his reputation.'

'His reputation for recklessness is already well-established. I would like him to enlarge his scholarship.' For a moment she was silent. 'His father wasn't a bad King for lack of bravery but for lack of wisdom. His son could do so much better, if he applied himself.'

'Warships,' said the captain, staring through the rain at the small harbor of Agdir. 'And not King's ships either, not with those red sails.'

'Let's stay outside,' said Muus. 'We must send a scout in first.'

'Me,' said Hraab. 'Tonight, after dark. Just like in Nidros, they'll never notice me.'

Muus hesitated. 'I don't like it, but all right.'

'Whoop,' said the boy happily. 'The ship's boat can drop me on that little bit of beach over there. From there, I'll swim to the boat stairs halfway that quay.'

'You sound like a spy,' said Birthe.

Hraab gave her an innocent stare. 'I? No, I'm not old enough. I'm just very good at creeping.'

'At least you can do something,' said Prince Ottil, and his eyes were angry. 'Heaps of people want to kill me and I can do nothing.'

'Your time will come.' Hraab poked his shoulder. 'Come, we'll read that terribly dull book of yours together.'

'A strange kid,' said the captain. 'Is he really as young as he looks?'

Muus stared after the two departed boys. 'He's very wise for his age. But I wonder about his family.'

As soon as it was dark, the captain had the ship's boat lowered. 'Anything you especially wanted to know?' said Hraab.

'Whose ships they are, whether the town is safe; anything about Queen Leocastre and Rannar would be welcome.'

Before Muus had finished his 'Be careful', the boy had disappeared into the night. Not long afterwards, they heart the soft splash of oars in the water, as two sailors rowed him to the tiny beach.

'Where is he?' The paladin's voice was full of barely suppressed rage.

'Who? Hraab?'

She made a furious gesture. 'Ottil. He isn't in his berth.'

'He won't be walking the ship in the pitch dark,' said Muus. Then he looked toward the harbor. 'He wouldn't...'

For once since they'd known her, the paladin cursed.

'Careful,' said Hraab. 'Don't go stompin' around, we're spies, not soldiers. Just act like an ordinary kid and remember, if a sailor asks who we are, we're from the town. If it's a townsman, we're from the ships. Clear?'

'Of course.'

'Right then. We'll have to swim to the stairs, they're over yonder.'

'Swim? Ehh, mate, I can't swim.'

'Oh. Well, I'll have to drag you along then. Come one and don't panic.'

'I never panic,' said Ottil. 'Princes don't.'

'Hold on to that.' Hraab waded into the water. 'Now come over here. On your back, you must float, like you're dead. Keep your mouth closed. Ready?'

'Yes,' said the Prince, sounding muffled but calm.

Hraab gripped the other's chin and pressed Ottil's head to his chest. Then, swimming steadily, he pulled the other boy along to the stone stairs. The Prince kept word and didn't panic. The only sound he made when they were at the stairs, was a soft sigh.

'Up,' said Hraab. 'And remember, act normal.'

Ottil nodded.

It was quiet in the town, as if everyone kept to themselves. The only folks they saw were near the great hall in the center. Locals, mostly, talking in hushed tones with each other. As the boys neared, they shut up and moved away, as if afraid to be overheard.

Hraab looked at his companion and shrugged. Then, with a face as innocent as a newborn puppy, he slipped past the slightly ajar doors into the hall. Here the boys stood for a moment, dripping as if soaked by the rain outside. They looked around through the smoke and the noise, the smell of beer and the burning torches. The hall was packed with sailors and fighters, with drinkers, gamblers and dancers to the sound of flutes and horns. They weren't Nords, more like the men Vulf and Swinne had with them, Fynni warriors. As two gawking kids, the boys wandered through the throng, catching a word here, snatching a sentence there. These men served some nameless Warlord. And Jarl Rannar was on his way to Nidros, to take the Crown and be guardian of the young Prince Ottil. The Prince gripped Hraab's arm when they heard this, his hand was rock-still, but his fingers bit hard.

'Not a man here is sober enough to appear before the Warlord,' said a gruff voice close by.

'When one uses wildmen, one has to get used to their wild ways.' The second voice sounded tired. 'I'm fed up with these barbarians.'

'Me too, Lendmann, drunken, murdering beasts they are.' Suddenly the gruff voice said almost in their ears, 'Hey, you boys. Come here.'

Hraab looked up. The speaker was a tall soldier, armed in mail. 'You're locals, aren't you?'

'Yes, Lord,' said Hraab, looking straight at the man as a free lad would.

'I need one to bring a message to someone important. Interested?'

Hraab cocked his head. 'Does it pay, Lord?'

The tall man roared with laughter. 'You've got your wits on you, I say that. Yes, it'll pay.'

'Then we'll deliver the message. What does it say?'

'Oh no, it's not a spoken message, kid. It's secret, written on parchment. You won't be able to read it. Just deliver it to the Warlord on board the merchant ship in the harbor. He'll pay you.'

Hraab nodded. 'We'll be careful with your secret, Lord.'

'You'd better', growled the big man. 'There are great happenings at stake here.' From his inside his tunic he took a folded document.

'Is this wise?' said the tired voice next to him, a young man dressed like a noble warrior.

'There is no-one else, Lord Thorgild.' The big soldier rubbed his face. 'The Warlord needs the letter now. I can't send one of those fools here, you know how he thinks of drunkenness, and you and I must go after the lady immediately.' He turned to Hraab. 'Here, take this and be quick about it. Tell the Warlord it's from Jorgard.'

'Yes, Lord,' said Hraab, and to Ottil: 'Come, I'll race you to the ship.'

Outside the hall, they ran towards the harbor. After two streets, Hraab halted. He looked around but there was nobody. Then he took the message from his tunic and unfolded it. 'These aren't runes. It's the same patter as that book of yours. I can't read it.'

'Give it to me.' Ottil took the letter. 'That's Old Romic, what the scribes in Gaul use.' While he read, he gasped and stared at Hraab. 'My mother... They were after my mother. She has fled Ejrikastelle. They have captured the royal Hold. That bastard Rannar wants to marry her. *Rannar* as my father? Never!'

'We must hurry. Let's bring this letter to the man in the ship and go back to the *Madgund.* Come, run.'

Only one ship in the harbor was larger than all the others, so there they went. At the gangway they were halted by a burly warrior, a Nord.

'Go play somewhere else, boys, no place for kids.'

'We bring a message for the Warlord, from Jorgard.'

'A message, hey? And why didn't Jorgard send one of 'is own men?'

Hraab leaned forward. 'Drunk, all of them,' said he confidentially.

The warrior laughed. 'Lucky bastards. Well, get yourselves on board. And mind yer manners, the Warlord is really a big man.'

They were right. A sailor brought them aft, where a part of the aftercastle was shut off by waxed cloth. 'Messenger for you, Lord,' said the man without entering.

'Send him in, man.' The voice was deep and impatient, and for a moment Ottil's hand gripped Hraab's arm like a bear trap. Then the boys entered.

Seated on a wooden chest was a large man; large by Nordic standards, with broad shoulders, and a strangely wrought helmet that covered most of his face.

He turned his head to stare at the two boys. 'Messenger? You two?'

'Yes, Lord,' said Hraab. 'Ban is my name and this is my cousin Ralf. We bring you a message from Jorgard.'

The dark eyes behind the mask glistened. 'Why didn't Jorgard come?'

'I believe he had to get away immediately, Lord. More I don't know.'

He held out the slightly damp parchment.

The Warlord took it and glanced over it. Then he swore. 'She's gone. By Thor, that woman is too smart to live. Of course Jorgard won't catch her. The bitch is on her way to Rhemes by now, with her lap dog Dettrich.' Then he remembered the boys. 'No matter,' said he in dismissal. 'You've done your duty, thank you.'

Hraab hesitated. 'Lord?'

The Warlord turned an impatient face his way. 'What?'

'Jorgard said that you'd pay us, Lord.'

The big man relaxed and he laughed. 'You're a clever one, lad.' He pulled a large pouch from his belt and took out two silver coins. 'Here, one each. Now be off with you.'

'Thank you, Lord,' said Hraab, and they hurried from the makeshift cabin.

'He was in a good mood?' The warrior at the gangway winked. 'I heard him laugh.'

'He was,' said Hraab. 'Uncommonly handsome, too. A great man, this Warlord.'

'He is, be sure he is.'

The boys ran off, skipping past a young man walking up the gangway without really seeing him. 'Another messenger?' Hraab caught the warrior's words, but not the young man's answer. They turned into a side-street and, careful that no-one saw them, returned to the waiting ship's boat.

Tuuri stared at the fleet moored in Agdir's harbor. They were Rannar's ships, with the same red sails as his own. And there, riding at anchor just out of the bay, was the merchant ship they'd been following from Nidros.

'Do you want us to enter harbor?' said the skipper.

Tuuri looked up from his thoughts. 'The quicker I'll make my report, the better.'

Half an hour later he walked down the quay, towards the town. The weather was clear and compared to where he came from, mild, but still there was almost no-one in the streets. The few people he saw looked taut, almost apprehensive, as if Agdir was occupied by an enemy army.

He came to the mead hall in the center, a large building, as was fitting for a rich port. He entered and froze. *Fynni*. No wonder the people looked afraid, Rannar had brought a few hundred murderous Fynni warriors with him.

Tuuri looked around, trying to see if Rannar was here, but most of the men were bigger than him and they blocked his view the ones still standing, at least, for the warriors had been celebrating, and were as drunk as Swinne's men at Belisheim. He weaved his way through them, disregarding their stupid jokes and name-calling. Nowhere was a glimpse of an officer or lord, let alone the Jarl. Trying to remain as inconspicuous as possible, he worked his way back to the exit. Once outside, he wiped his head. Two townsmen stood nearby, looking at him, but they didn't say anything. Their eyes betrayed them, though. They were hostile, fearful and suspicious.

'Pardon,' Tuuri said, 'could you tell me where to find the Warlord?'

The men just stared. Never before had Tuuri felt hated in his own country, but now he wanted to flee, to hide.

Finally, one of the men pointed towards the harbor.

'Thank you.' Then he blurted, 'Don't look at me like that. I didn't bring those Fynni here.'

Silence. Then the man tapped his left cheek.

Tuuri blanched. His mark! They thought him one of those beasts. He realized he was branded for life and with a sob he fled.

Once back at the harbor, he had regained his composure. The first and largest ship had a guard at the entry port, so that's where he went. At the gangway he nearly walked into two boys coming from the ship. They didn't really see him but he recognized them immediately.

'Who are you?' said the guard. 'Not another messenger?'

On deck, a Fynni soldier brought him to a makeshift cabin aft. 'Messenger for you, Lord.'

'Let him come back this afternoon,' said a voice from within. 'I'm engaged now.'

Tuuri hesitated, but the soldier gave him no chance. 'Come away, the Warlord has no time for you, Fynnikin.'

'The Prince is here!' he shouted, but the soldier slapped his face and dragged him to the railing. 'Don't shout. Come back this afternoon.'

The guard grinned. 'Those Fynni are direct bastards. But then, you're one of them, aren't you?'

'No!' Tuuri spat the word out. 'I'm not!'

Aboard the *Madgund,* the stress was mounting with the passing of the hours. The paladin had totally lost her air of frigid rectitude, pacing the deck and muttering dire promises at the address of the absent Prince.

'Don't worry,' said Ajkell. 'They'll be back.'

'They're just children.' The paladin turned around and waved her fists. 'They will be killed, or sold in slavery.'

'Why? That they're children is their protection. And Hraab is a shrewd lad. He's been living in the woods for nearly a month, all alone, following that bastard Vulf and his ulvhednar. If he can survive that, a short trip to Agdir won't bother him.'

'Boat ahoy.' shouted a sailor, and he threw down a rope ladder.

The paladin rushed to the gangway. 'You.' Her gloved hand pointed at the Prince as he climbed back on board. 'How dare you leave the ship without my permission? I'll have you thrashed, young man, I'll make you regret your waywardness.

'The Prince wasn't in danger,' said Hraab seriously. 'He really, really wasn't. But he's so full of anger that he had to do something and better this than something foolish.'

Ottil's face was red and furious and it was doubtful if he had heard the paladin's tirade. 'That bastard,' said he, 'that cowardly, rat-bitten, dung-eating dog.'

'Quite,' said Ajkell. 'Who?'

'Rannar.'

The bear warrior stiffened. 'Are those Rannar's ships?'

Hraab nodded. 'He wore a fancy mask and called himself the Warlord. But at Rannar's only visit to court our Royal friend here had been playing spy on his father once, hiding behind a curtain, and he recognized the Jarl immediately. He was very clever at keeping his mouth shut, too.'

'He was after my mother,' shouted Ottil. He wrestled visibly with his self-control as he told of their mission. 'So there he sat, the smug white-haired, rotten poxhound. A bitch, he called her. My mother the Queen, a bitch. And then he paid us. After Hraab had reminded him.'

He turned to Hraab. 'Where is that second coin?' he snapped. 'It's mine.'

With a show of reluctance, Hraab handed him the silver piece. 'Here, I thought Princes were rich.'

'Perhaps other Princes are,' said Ottil. 'But I'm not.' He turned to his tutor, his face stiff. 'I heard your words, paladin. You overstep your authority as my tutor. You are to teach me my letters, not to curb me in my duties. I will no longer be treated as a child. I haven't got the time for it. I must recover my kingdom. With my father dead and my mother gone I must be a man now.' He gave her a hard stare. 'I will not be thwarted, paladin.'

The paladin looked at him, her face unreadable. 'You claim a lot of responsibility, Prince Ottil. If that is your wish, prove to us your manhood, as is the custom.'

'But not now,' said Birthe from behind. 'You two get off to bed. You've had a busy night.'

Hraab nodded. 'You're right. Come on, Prince, I'm tired.'

The paladin let her shoulders sag. 'I shouldn't have been so tactless. His manhood. He's only twelve.'

'It is his right,' said Ajkell gravely. 'Nor is it unique. Remember the tales of Young Grimmor the Red and of Boar-Anulf. The latter was even younger than Ottil when he killed his first man.'

'They died young, too,' said the paladin bitterly.

The bear warrior shrugged. 'That's Fate.'

'I'm not cut out for this task.' Valiantrude sighed. 'I'm a warrior, not a wet nurse. He is a good lad, Ottil, but he has outlived my patience years ago. I wish I could resign this duty.'

The captain had seen to the stowing of the ship's boat and now he joined them. 'So my Queen fled,' said he. 'She's a resourceful woman. What will you do now?'

'Our orders are to bring Ottil to his mother,' said Kjelle with a frown.

'If she's indeed gone to Rhemes, then we must go there.'

'Rhemes, pearl of Gaul.' The captain sounded a bit nostalgic. 'Long time since I was there. I can sail you to Harflot, no farther.' He shook his head. 'I'm not going to make a profit on this journey.'

Birthe smiled at him. 'Well, you can ask King Leodowric for compensation. After all, you're transporting his nephew to safety.'

Gunthram's face brightened. 'Leodowric is an honorable man; he will see the fairness of my claim.'

That afternoon, Tuuri went back to the Jarl's ship and this time he was admitted into his master's presence. Rannar sat at ease on a large chest and regarded him with pursed lips. 'So there you are. You took your time, I must say.'

'Your pardon, Lord, but things are not going well in the North.' He hesitated, before blurting out. 'Lord, I wanted to warn you, but they wouldn't let me near you. Prince Ottil was here.'

Rannar's eyebrows rose. 'Are you mad? Ottil is safely in the north.'

Tuuri shook his head. 'No, Lord, he's not. He escaped. And today he was here, together with a second boy.'

'Those lads? They were locals, bringing me word from hirdman Jorgard.' Rannar's eyes were chilly. 'You seem overwrought. Won't you rather lie down and return another time?'

Tuuri shocked upright. 'No, Lord, I want to make my report.'

The Jarl sighed. 'Well, then do so.'

Tuuri stood at attention, hands on his back, and recounted everything he had seen and done from the moment he first landed in Helmshaven.

Rannar clasped his hands around a knee, listening, looking at him, his eyes unreadable.

Tuuri finished and stood there, silently waiting for his master's outburst. But none came. The Jarl nodded slowly. 'Thank you. A clear report, young man. Now I'll think up new orders for you. Go and wait outside, will you.'

'But, Lord... Prince Ottil...'

'I heard you. Did you hear me?'

'Yes, Lord,' said Tuuri crestfallen. 'I'll wait outside.'

'The Shardheld.' From the other side of the canvas screen of the cabin came a tall man. His hair was long, his forehead high and his eyes glittered under heavy ridges. His face bore many of the worst Fynni markings. 'If that fool boy spoke the truth, this could make you mighty beyond belief, Jarl.'

Rannar stared at his Fynni advisor. 'How so?'

'You know the saga of the Shardheld?'

'Of course.'

'Then think. The skyshard contains a duplicate of all the magic in the world. Should it fall into your hands, it would give you all that power. At the same time, all the Wisewomen and priests in the world will lose their arts. You could dole it out to them on your conditions, Jarl. You could have them all working for you.'

Rannar sat back on his chest, mulling it over. 'There is wisdom in your words, Rev. How will I get this shard in my hands?'

The sa'aman's eyes caught Rannar's and the Jarl shivered. Rev's eyes held a peculiar light. A brooding, violent darklight, that always made him feel uncomfortable..

'You need the Shardheld to bring it to you, Jarl. Just capture him and bring him here. Unconscious, if you know what's good for you.'

Rannar felt the back of his head sting, as if a headache was lying in wait. One of those terrible headaches that plagued him more and more, these days. 'And how will I capture the Shardheld? Shall I send someone after him?'

'You won't get him by chasing him around the known world, Jarl. Catch the mouse at the mouse hole. There's only one entrance to Falrom, a certain mountain pass between Olhorec in Gaul and Utobrenno, the only village in Falrom. Place your men there and he'll walk right into your hands.'

'I'll send Vulf,' said Rannar. 'I'll write him new instructions.'

'A clever choice, Jarl. He's a tenacious chieftain.' With a bow, the sa'aman retired behind the sheets.

A soldier roused Tuuri from his thoughts. 'The Warlord wants you, Fynnikin. Hurry.'

Rannar sat as before, smiling at Tuuri as he came in.

'Your information caused a change of plan, young man. I want you to go north, with new instructions for Warchief Vulf. Prepare for a long journey, for you'll accompany him south again, to Gaul and beyond. This is your chance for glory, boy. Here are your orders. Do you need any money?'

The Jarl's command froze Tuuri's veins with dread. He was to go south with Vulf? That creepy murderer? He swallowed and thought of the gold pieces sewn into his mantle and nodded. 'I do, if it pleases you, Lord.'

Rannar reached behind him. 'Here, that should be sufficient. Now hurry, you have a ship to catch.'

'Thank you for your trust, Lord,' said Tuuri, pale faced. He groaned inwardly, what had been a boy's dream once, was now a heart-stopping nightmare. Silently, he bowed to his Lord and went back to his own ship.

Twelve nights since they left Agdir and the Norden, Muus woke as the *Madgund* rolled unexpectedly. The patter of bare feet running over his head sounded different from other nights, more urgent. After a while, he rose, careful not to wake any of the others, and went on deck. The predawn showed angry white-haired waves and the clouds overhead stormed past like a herd of maddened bison. The sailors worked feverishly, shortening the sail and checking the riggings, their faces worried. The captain greeted him with a strained expression. 'We're in for a blow, Runemaster,' said he. 'A big one. Unless you have tricks to abort a gale.'

'I'm afraid not. Where are we now?'

'Passing the Frysian coast. The wind is northeastern, and we'll not make Harflot, this way. We're blown towards the Brytan coast, clear across the Narrow Sea. I'm hoping to find shelter in a bay there, Njord willing.'

But Njord, Lord of Sea and Storm, wasn't cooperating. Relentlessly, his anger whipped sea and wind into a frenzy. The predawn proved a lie, no dawn was coming, only the clouds, and with them, the rain.

With her sail reefed, the *Madgund* wrestled her mighty opponent. Waves, topping the mast easily, lifted the ship, shook her and threw her down again in endless anger, but every time the little ship lifted her bow and plowed onward. Muus stood with his back to the mast, as he had done ten years ago, on Bearjaw's ship. Just like then, he wasn't afraid. The angry seas touched something deep inside him and filled every empty spot in his body with their rage. The day wore on without the wind abating. The seamen stopped their useless attempts and huddled together, awaiting the will of the Gods. Only the captain and his two helmsmen aft kept their hands on the tiller, trying to keep the *Madgund's* bow in the wind, meeting the waves head-on. Should the ship broach-to, catch the sea on her broadside, the force would keel her over and that would be the end of it. Muus stood as if nailed to the groaning mast, his eyes staring ahead. He saw not the foam whitening the deck, nor the clouds and the lightning. Round huts filled his mind, a placid river amidst rolling hills. Sheep grazing, little boys fishing from the green banks, men and women at work. Talking and laughing, their faces open and happy. Faces he knew, even if he couldn't remember their names. The men had long mustaches, but no beards, which gave them a curiously naked look after all his years amongst hairy Nords. A man with a long, red mantle over a white robe, his hair hanging over his shoulders; a woman, small, black-haired and beautiful, carrying an black-and-white kitten. They were people with faces, not the unrecognizable shapes from his dreams. Slowly, the storm blew the mists in his head away. *Terrel,* whispered the woman with the kitten. *Terrel,* called the man in the red mantle. *Terrel,* shouted the children. *Come home, Terrel. Come home now.* A loud, rending sound shocked him out of his dream. A tremor went through the ship, the deck buckled, the mast at his back swayed and toppled over the side. It all happened fast.

Kjelle saw Muus go overboard. 'No.' he shouted, his cry torn from his mouth by the wind. He rushed to the railing, but it was too dark to see. Another crash shook the ship and he saw the forecastle break loose and slide into the sea. Then the deck under his feet tore open and he dropped into the water-filled hold. The rim of a wooden drum struck the breath from his lungs and he swallowed dirty water. His knees touched a rocky surface and he managed to creep out of the hole in the side into the storm light. He looked around at the sea raging just a few feet away. Vague in the distance he thought he saw a coastline. *Brytanna?* he thought. Then a wave swept him from his perch. His hands touched a wooden surface and desperately he tried to get hold of it. It was the hatch door to the hold, and his hands found some grip. Using a lifting wave, he managed to climb on top of it.

'Help me up,' shouted a voice in the water. It was Birthe, her face a pale blob at the edge of the hatch. Hurriedly, Kjelle scrambled to her side. The hatch stamped and shook, but he managed to get the girl next to him.

'Are you all right?' he stammered, suddenly feeling cold and scared.

'We're alive,' said the girl.

'We?'

'Búi and I, of course.'

'Gods, the baby. Is he...?'

'Babies are like seals. Can stay under water longer than we. Only the cold is bad.' Then she started to cry. 'Freya help me, I'm so scared.'

'Me too,' said Kjelle. 'Dammit, I've been scared all my life. But now at least I've got a reason.'

Hours passed.

'Is the storm lessening or am I only hoping it?' Kjelle forced the words out from between salt-cracked lips.

'It is. See the bits of blue sky.'

'Don't dare to look up. Fingers so stiff, I'm afraid to lose my hold.' Kjelle coughed, spitting out seawater. 'Can't see if we're nearing the coast.'

Birthe said nothing, only Bui cried in his wet furs, eliciting answers from the wild gulls overhead.

A bump woke Kjelle from his exhausted numbness. He opened his red-rimmed eyes and stared in the beady eyes of a black-capped gull standing on a piece of flotsam that lay half on the beach and half in the water. 'Land,' he croaked. Then it penetrated through the fog in his head. 'Land.' He shook Birthe. 'A beach. We're saved.'

The girl turned her head. 'What?' Then she came to her knees and while baby Búi started to cry again, she sang of thanksgiving.

Kjelle stepped into the water and helped her climb down next to him. Then, arms around each other, they staggered onto the sandy beach.

The two boys clung to the railing of the *Madgund's* forecastle.

'We're not goin' to make it!' shouted Ottil against the wind. His face was purple from the cold and the lashing winds. The forecastle, a wooden platform independent of the ship's structure, shook alarmingly. A loud creaking sounded as one of its posts tore loose.

'Off! Jump to the deck!' said Hraab, his words ripped from his lips by the storm. He grabbed Ottil's arm and dragged the boy with him.

They were hardly down before the forecastle toppled into the sea. At the same moment, the deck started to buckle. Planking tore and a large hole filled with foaming water yawned at their feet.

'Ship's breaking up,' cried Ottil.

'Quick,' Hraab pointed to the forecastle, upside down in the sea a small leap away from them. 'That's our boat. Jump!'

They landed on the forecastle and fell as a large wave lifted them and bore them away from the ship. Just in time, for the entire nose of the *Madgund* disintegrated.

'Damn,' said Ottil, trying desperately not to scream.

Hraab put his arm around him and they huddled on their makeshift raft of the forecastle, cold and terrified, swept away by an angry sea into the night.

Muus came out of his stupor when the mast hit something. The heavy rear end dragged deeper in the water. Now it bumped once, twice, and then dragged. Rubbing the salt from his eyes with a nearly frozen hand, Muus stared ahead. It was much lighter now and through the spray he thought he saw hills. Not the green downs of his dreams, but rougher, like the coast near Harkoy. He sighed. Brytanna. He knew it was, the dream people had faces, a sign that his memory was returning. *Terrel.* The stone on his breast felt warm. It was still angry. Several times while he drifted it had tried to take over. It wanted to bring him to Falrom directly. He felt the skyshard react to his thought. *No. I'm not a slave. Not to Kjelle and not to you. I'll go when I'm ready.* The speed of the broken mast lessened, in spite of the tug of the incoming tide at his legs. Without a thought, he let go of the lines that had been his hold on the mast, and pushed away. With weak, stiff strokes, he swam towards the hills, carried by the tide, until his feet touched a graveled bottom. Then he stood, only to fall down again. Slowly he rose and stumbled through the rough surf towards the stony beach.

GLOSSARY

Alf = the originals of those we now call elves.
Bondsman = a freeman who is a farmer or artisan
Draug = a walking dead. (plural: draugar)
Freedman = a former slave now freed
Freeman = a freeborn Nord (male or female)
Fynni = a shamanic people of the Nordish Ostmark
Fynnikin = half-breed Fynni/Ostmarker
Headman = captain of a Hold's warriors
Hirdman = a (high-ranking) personal follower of a king/jarl
Hold = the property of a Holder
Holder = Nordish rank, lord of a Hold
Holderling = the male heir of a Hold
Karl = a freeman who is both farmer and fighter
Lendmann = a rank of councilor to king or jarl
Lightalves = golden haired alves (hist.)
Long Night, the = Polar Night, the
Rest = a measure of distance: a two-hour walk
Runemaster = a man practicing runemagic (high level)
Sa'aman = a shamanic priest of the Fynni
Sa'amaniman = the shamanic chief priest of the Fynni
Svartalves = dark-haired alves (hist.)
Tarkynn = a Fynni warleader
Thrall = a slave
Ulvhednar = Fynni wolf berserkers (singular & plural)
Völva = a woman practicing seidr magic (high level)
Wise(wo)man = a person practicing magic (low level)

LIST OF NAMES

Ajkell Gudrofsen, bear warrior
Alman, Holder of Eidungruve; Kjelle's father
Asgisla, Völva of Belisheim
Barn (D), Birthe's first husband, Búi's father
Birthe Gudesdotter; Pupil to Asgisla
Brundal, Jarl; Landesregent
Búi Birthesen, Birthe's baby son
Darh the Bashing Wind (Sky), a God Before
Dettrich, Jarl of Dalland
Elward, watchman of Eidungruve
Ema, Kjelle's amour
Frey, Nordic/Gaullish God of male magic
Freya, Nordic/Gaullish Goddess of female magic
Gude the Viking, Birthe's father
Gunthchramn, captain of the *Madgund*
Hagen (D), a warrior of Eidungruve
Harald Enske, foreman of Eidungruve
Harbard, a one-eyed man
Hel, Nordic/Gaullish Goddess of the Afterlife, Helheim
Hilde Luofsdotter, Largassen's wife
Hraab , scavenger of the dead
Jal (-with-the-Fine-Boots), a warrior of Eidungruve
Jorgard, a hirdman in Jarl Rannar's service.
Kimbel, Bearjaw's Un-a-Dach slave clerk
Kjelle Almansen; Holderling of Eidungruve
Leocastre, Queen of the Norden, mother to Ottil
Leodowric, King of Gaul
Logmar, one of King Vidmer's Lendmenn
Matta, elderly maid of Largassen Bearjaw
Meili Brandrsen (D), Holderling of Leidwald
Muus, body slave to Holderling Kjelle
Niord (Stiller-of-Storms), Nordic God of Sea and Storms
Odin, the Allfather, chief God of the Nordic pantheon
Orn the Red, a warrior of Eidungruve
Orwang the Drowner Giant (Sea), a God Before
Ottil Vidmersen, Prince of the Norden

Radgundis de Megern, wife to Dettrich Jarl of Dalland
Rannar Walesen , (Snake), Jarl of Westhal
Rev, the Sa'amaniman, the Fynni chief priest.
Sha'akaii, Tuuri's totem bear
Siga, Wisewoman of Eidungruve
Skid Largassen Bearjaw, the Viking of Helmshaven
Swanfrid (D), Holddaughter of Jonthal; Meili's bride
Swinne, follower of Rannar, a Fynni tarkynn
Thor, Nordic/Gaullish God of War and Battle
Thorgild Thorgildsen, Lord, Lendmann to Rannar
Tuuri Little Knife, Rannar's messenger
Urus the Destroyer (Earth), a God Before
Valiantrude de Vergy, Paladin of the Court of Gaul
Vidmer II; King of de Norden; Ottil's father
Vulf, follower of Rannar, a Fynni tarkynn
Waldrich, Jarl of Herigel
Walther, procurateur for Radgundis of Dalland

AUTHOR'S LETTER

Dear Reader,

Thank you for reading my work.

I hope you found as much enjoyment in it as I found in writing the story. If not, I apologize for failing you...

I have a request.

Would you, dear Reader, tell the world whether you liked this book or not?

If so, would you write a small review of it at Amazon, Smashwords, Goodreads or wherever you bought it?

Should you like the story, I won't mind your jubilant opinion. And if you don't, well, I'll hope you won't hesitate to say so. Perhaps then I can do better next time. Positive or negative, your opinion is of great value to me.

And should you have any questions about the book or the story, you can always find me at pehorsman@gmail.com. I promise to answer any questions you might have.

Thank you for your input!

Paul E. Horsman

RHIDAUNA

If you enjoyed this book, perhaps you would be interested in my other fantasy adventure, The Shadow of the Revenaunt-series:

Driven from his home by terrible monsters, Ghyll Denhalf sets out into the world. Spurred on by his desperate oath of revenge, the young man must find out who is behind the attacks that killed his family and that terrorize the land of Rhidauna. With assassins and dark mages on his heels, he travels with his friends all over the kingdom and beyond, fighting and dodging death. After surviving many dangers he finally reaches his destination, only to be imprisoned by the very powers he serves...

To give you a taste, here are the first pages of Rhidauna, The Shadow of the Revenaunt, Chapter 1, in which Ghyll, his foster brother Olle and their friend Damion leave their home, Castle Tinnurad, to go on an illicit boar hunt. Ghyll knows well his uncle and guardian, Baron Jadron Halwyrd, won't be happy with their adventure, but the need to prove himself is stronger than his usual caution...

CHAPTER 1 - BOAR HUNT

Four times the bronze voice of the tower bell rang out over the courtyard. At the first note, the lads ducked into the shadows and stared at the rain-drenched square. Minutes passed without anyone appearing.

Ghyll Denhalf threw the other two a triumphant grin; everything was going as planned. The night watchmen, all ancient veterans, found the weather too miserable to man the walls. They would be sitting by the fire in the Guardhouse, their boots at the door and their weapons stacked in the rack, while they killed the time with mulled wine, dice and the retelling of their war stories. The lads' way was clear.

The three slipped through the open gate into the darkness beyond. The world outside the walls lay wrapped in rain; nothing moved but the falling water. Four hours past midnight and castle Tinnurad slept.

Without speaking, they hurried to the stable at the castle farm, where their horses stood. Their trained fingers found saddle straps and buckles by touch and soon they led the animals away. In the boathouse at the breakwater, the barge waited and moments later, they sailed on their adventure.

'We did it!' Ghyll took a deep breath, gazing in the direction of the invisible mainland. He knew his foster brother's eyes were on his back, so he chuckled. Olle didn't approve of this clandestine enterprise, but he followed Ghyll's lead, as he always did. And Damion? The new lad went along because he had asked him.

In the distance loomed the dark mass of the Dar Traun. To Ghyll it felt as if the mountain waited for them. We're coming, he thought, curbing his impatience. Since his uncle's forester told him there were boar higher up the slope of the Traun, Ghyll knew he had to kill one for his twentieth birthday, tomorrow. He had a vague notion that coming of age and hunting boar belonged together, as if one would prove his fitness for the other. He grunted. Uncle Jadron would not be pleased they had gone out without permission. But the urge was irresistible.

An hour later, they were in the field at the foot of the Traun, on the overlook above the river. Ghyll gazed up at the darkened summit. Am I mad? His chest tightened. I can't do this! He was about to turn away. They'd go home, back to bed, they... His foster brother slammed the gate shut and the crash sent his doubts fleeing into the night. He sucked the moist, pine-scented air deep into his lungs and swung his arms a few times to make his blood run faster. The tension drained from his body. Come on, faint heart; the swine are waiting!

Ulanth, Uncle Jadron's warhorse, turned one lazy eye on him. Then it pulled a tuft of grass from the ground and started to chew, imperturbable as ever. Ghyll patted the animal's neck, before handing his spear to Olle. He inspected the small paddock where they would leave their mounts. With the gate closed, everything looked safe. 'Ready, lads?'

Olle nodded, but Damion's answer sounded so hesitant, that Ghyll frowned. More nerves? He turned away and faced the mountain. 'Let's go, then.'

The hunter's trail that led them upwards through the pinewoods was muddy but passable. Not for long, though. After a few bends, the forest grew closer, the ground more slippery, and the visibility worse. Without talking, they walked through the near dark, until a rustling in the undergrowth brought them to an abrupt halt. Ghyll's hand went to his hunting knife, but he relaxed again as a rabbit fled across the path. Behind him, Olle chuckled.

Ghyll bristled. Does he think I'm afraid? For a moment, he stood still, listening to the sounds of the forest. From somewhere in front of them came the secretive sound of snapping twigs. Farther away among the trees a hunting owl called, ominous in the lightlessness of the woods. Ghyll felt a shiver run down his spine.

They hurried on, trying to stay on the path in the dark. Next to him, Damion muttered something under his breath and the set of his shoulders betrayed his dislike of the forest. Ghyll couldn't blame him; he didn't enjoy the watching pines and the rain-filled silence either. Without thinking, he whistled a few bars of a battle song. but stopped abruptly. Nonsense, they're just trees on a mountain!

Behind his back, Olle scraped his throat. 'Why the hurry?'

Ghyll slowed down. 'All right, all right. If you can't keep up...'

Olle sang in an undertone. 'Sa, Ballady with mighty sword, hit out at all and sundry,' the same air Ghyll had whistled. 'You're right, it is a bit creepy here.'

Ghyll laughed. Even my tough brother feels uneasy. For a while, his mood lightened.

Soon the trail came to a dead end. The days-long rain must have caused a landslide, for a mass of mud and stones barred their way. Without thinking, Ghyll led them to the left, until they reached a small stream. Here they went uphill, slipping on the loose gravel in the bed.

To Ghyll's surprise, Damion seemed uncomfortable with the climb through the fast-flowing creek. Ghyll didn't know the other lad well enough yet. Damion had come to live at castle Tinnurad a tennight ago and Uncle Jadron expected his nephew to keep an eye on the newcomer. Ghyll grinned. That's why Damion was out here with them, in the rain, trudging up a mountain.

'Your father was Sergeant of the Guard at Halwyrd?'

The lad nodded.

Ghyll glanced sideways. 'I heard you trained with Halwyrds soldiers?'

The other just stared straight ahead, splashing through the ankle high water.

'This mustn't be difficult for you, then. With a father like that...'

'Enough about my father. I hate him!'

'Oh!' Ghyll looked at the lad in surprise. 'Why?'

Damion shook his head and they plodded on in silence.

When the gray dawn broke, they had reached a field full of dead trees. Barkless trunks grew like withered limbs out of the haze which breathed from the rocky surface. The lads looked at each other.

'Eerie,' said Olle.

Ghyll nodded. It seemed as if the Underworld reached into the plane of Life here, and made the land die a slow death. Uncertain, he looked around. Which way should they go? He saw past the sulphurised tree trunks the contours of an ancient temple and his heart grew cold with horror. Stone arms arose in a circle against the night sky, each more than five man-lengths tall, with hands clawing at the heavens, as if wanting to tear the universe asunder. Those hands! Now Ghyll knew where they were. 'Tilia!' he muttered. 'Why do you bring us here?' He studied the surroundings, but they could not avoid the ruins. The temple lay wedged between rock wall and precipice and the one possible route upwards led them through the sinister shrine.

As they got closer, Ghyll's repulsion grew, as if something dreadful was waiting for them in the temple. A presence that knew them and followed their every move. He tried not to look at the center of the temple, but to no avail: the effigy of a four-armed deity drew his gaze thither. The idol squatted on a pedestal at a stained altar. Wind and weather had worn away its features, but the crude, female form emanated so much evil, that Ghyll muttered a curse. Something woke up and moved between the reaching arms. A mass of black creatures fled over their heads, winging towards the sky.

Damion jumped. 'Monsters!'

'They're just bats, lad.' said Olle.

'Drat it, they startled me!' Damion looked rather sheepish. 'Where are we?'

'Where we shouldn't have been.' Ghyll took a deep breath, and his voice sounded calmer than he was. 'This is the Annan-ad-Aghraim.' He knew the old temple only from the tales of the soldiers and the servants at the castle and every story was the same. Long ago, in the Revenaunt Emperor's time, dark priests had performed gruesome rituals amid these stone arms. He shuddered, as if he still could feel the power coming from the faceless idol. *The boy is useless,* a voice whispered in his ear. *Offer him to me.* A silent, mocking laughter followed, and the tension between the grasping columns became almost palpable.

'Hey!' Damion sounded exited. 'See the animal pictures on this pillar.'

Ghyll turned around. 'Don't touch!'

It was too late.

Damion snatched his hand away from the relief in the pillar. 'Why not?'

Ghyll opened his mouth, but Olle was first. His foster brother grabbed the smaller lad by the shoulders and shook him, his face dark with anger. 'We're in a temple of the Revenaunt, idiot! Touching anything here gives bad luck. Didn't they ever teach you that?'

The lad hung his head. 'Yes. I'm sorry; it just happened.'

'Mainal aid me.' Olle let go of the other. 'Fool!'

Ghyll stared at the image Damion had touched, an ancient carving in the crude but unmistakable shape of a boar. 'Of all the bad luck... Enough, let's get away from here.'

Without another word, they fled up the mountain slope. *Hurry,* called the taunting thought of the idol after Ghyll. *Your prey is waiting for you!*

Once past the dead wood, they left the sulfuric fumes behind them as well. Relieved, they walked on between slender birches and more than man-high, blooming rhododendrons.

Their only warning was the sound of the danger itself, a shriek of madness that had them going for their weapons. Showering blossoms, a wild boar crashed through the bushes and blocked their path.

'Stand still!' The sweat broke Ghyll out at the sight of the monster. He had thought to find them a young male, inexperienced as themselves, not the massive champion of swine confronting them, with its raised bristles and spittle-stained tusks.

The beast paused for a moment and peered around with myopic eyes. It was so close, that Ghyll saw the hot breath steaming from its nostrils.

Damion took a step backwards. The boar yelled his fury and threw himself like a two hundred pound battering ram at the lad. That it didn't gut Damion on the spot was pure luck, for with that first, fatal step, a root caught the lad's heel and he landed flat on his back in the mud. Thus, the boar's left tusk missed his stomach and opened the lad's leg to the bone instead. Damion screamed once.

Olle threw Ghyll one of the two spears he carried, and buried the other one with a wild 'Ayooo' in the animal's flank. The boar turned with incredible speed to this new enemy. At the same time, Ghyll leapt forward and rammed his spear with all his weight behind it in the beast's chest. Again the boar turned, roaring its rage through the forest, and tore the shaft from Ghyll hands. Cursing, the lad clawed for his hunting knife. With all the energy he had left, he thrust the weapon deep in the boar's larynx and jumped back. Blood and foam splashed around. Once more, the creature reared up, shaking its head as if in denial and fell down dead. On top of Damion.

The lads heard a heartbreaking sound of snapping bones and they sprang forwards to pull the heavy carcass off their companion. Damion lay motionless, his eyes half closed; his face deadly pale and wet with rain.

'Gods, oh Gods.' Ghyll laid his aching fingers on the lad's carotid. For a long moment, he felt nothing, and his own breathing seemed to stop. Then he caught a far, faint beating. 'He's alive!'

The lads knew what to do. Ad nauseam, the fighting instructor had repeated it: take care of the victim's safety, sew up open wounds, and carry the victim to the nearest healing master. Since that time, Olle, the more cool-headed of the two of them, always carried a few needles and a ball of catgut. Now he sat on his knees in the mud, sewing with a steady hand the edges of the leg wound together.

'Bless the Gods the beast tore no artery. The leg's not bleeding much.'

'No, but his ribs...' Ghyll pursed his lips, while the cold fear swept through his body. With his knife, he began to cut his cloak into long strips, which he bound tightly around Damion chest.

When he had tied the last knot, they wrapped the unconscious lad in his own cloak. 'That's the best we can do.' Olle flexed his muscles and lifted Damion almost without effort from the ground. Then they began the long descent to the horses in the overlook field. It was as if the Gods had them by the hand, because they found a faster way down, making them avoid the sinister temple. Even then, it was a long walk and after a while, Olle's face began to purple.

Halfway, Ghyll looked up. 'Should I carry him for a bit?'

Olle shook his head. 'I can manage.'

'It's all my fault.' Ghyll was near to weeping. 'Me and my brilliant ideas. We shouldn't have come without drivers and dogs. '

His foster brother grunted something unintelligible, while the rain ran down his head and shoulders.

Once they arrived at the horses, Olle deposited the wounded lad on the ground and dropped beside him. 'Hold on... have to catch my breath.'

Ghyll nodded. 'He's still alive. Gods, what a mess!'

Olle lay sprawled on the grass and did not answer.

Ghyll wandered around, his mind lost in a chaos of remorse, fear, and a bitter anger of his own folly. At the brink of the cliff, he halted. In sudden desperation, he hit his fist against the trunk of the birch tree next to him and swore. Then he froze. Pieces of the rocky edge at his feet broke off and rained into the depths. He didn't notice it. Bewildered, he stared at the Yanthe below him. He rubbed his face with his cold hands, but the images refused to go. Beneath him, three phantoms sailed past through the rain; gray sea dragons, harbingers of misdoings. Ghyll watched them open-mouthed until they disappeared behind the river's bend. Drakenboats? Had he seen them or was it his imagination? The last time there'd been pirates on the river, was eighty years ago, and now...

'What's wrong?'

Ghyll pulled his curls. 'There aren't any Drakenlander raiding anymore... But I just saw three of their boats sailing past, towards Tinnurad.' He felt panic rising and clenched his fists. 'Let's go on!'

Olle came to his feet and moved his shoulders a few times. 'I'm ready.'

They strapped the unconscious Damion over Ulanth's neck. Then, leading their horses, they went home. On foot, the way back took hours. The pale circle of the sun behind the clouds betrayed that it was already past noon when they returned at the Yanthe Wachter, the old tower whence they could see Tinnurad...